A Ship in the Harbor

by Mary Heron Dyer

PARADIGM
Publishing
Company

San Diego, California

Cover Design by Hummingbird Graphics
Book Design and Typesetting by Paradigm Publishing

Printed in the United States on acid free paper

Excerpts from the song "Lullaby" reprinted with the kind permission of Cris Williamson

Library of Congress Catalog Card Number: 93-84467
ISBN 1-882587-00-6

A Ship in the Harbor

by Mary Heron Dyer

Mary Heron Dyer

Dedication

To H.N.C.—you let me go with your blessings when it was time for me to sail on the open seas to a destination I could only dream.

To my children—Ann, David, and Meg—may the wind fill your sails and speed you on your way.

To Vilik—my loving companion on the voyage.

May we all find safe harbor where we can rock on the waters and where choirs of angels sing us to sleep.

1
A Midsummer's Night

The mid-July day was overcast, and a hint of ocean breeze left a salt tang in the air. Directions in one hand, Oregon highway map spread out on the seat beside her, Meg tried to negotiate the snail-paced, bumper-to-bumper chain of cars winding south along the coast. "Tourists . . . ," she mumbled under her breath. "Weekenders." The ultimate local put-down. Then she laughed. She'd been a tourist herself until a couple of months ago, when she had found a run-down cabin she could afford. It felt good to laugh, although she wished she had a map to her own life as clear as the one beside her.

Meg was certain it was neither accident nor impulse that had brought her to the coast. It was freedom, a new beginning, the culmination of a spark kindled more than three years ago when she finally realized why she had sexual "problems" with her husband. She had picked frequent fights to keep him at a distance, without understanding why. It had taken over 15 years of marriage for her to discover that she was a lesbian, not just a frigid straight woman. In some ways, learning it had been the easy part.

She had fallen madly, totally in love with a lesbian already in a relationship. Too naive to recognize a sure recipe for trouble, Meg had hung on for over a year, agreeing to meet in secret and hide their relationship from everyone except, ironically enough, her husband.

It had been a year of clandestine meetings and public lies, a year of Meg shoring up Kim's eroded self-esteem and trying to help her believe she deserved more than an alcoholic, abusive partner. But when Cheryl agreed to go into treatment, Kim dropped Meg with no more than a phone call. Meg's new lesbian life came crashing down around her ears.

The thought of not having Kim in her life was so painful Meg had tried to keep a friendship going . . . until the day Kim showed up an hour late for a lunch date, arrogant and unapologetic, in the company of another woman Meg had never met. Protector? Witness? Replacement? Angry, hurting, Meg knew she had to let go of the friendship, too.

"Damn!" Meg reached up, suddenly glad the traffic was so slow, and wiped away the tears those memories still triggered. She had cried enough for that woman. Her very survival depended on cutting all ties.

Through all of that affair, Meg had lived at home with her husband, Mark, and their three kids: Alyson, now 16; Tom, 15; and Stacey, just turned 9. She had always lived with someone, going from living at home to a marriage at 18. Then she hadn't wanted to move away from Mark until Kim was ready to live with her. But after the breakup, she knew it was time to build her own nest, not just move into and re-line someone else's.

She left a 17-year marriage and the home she and Mark had bought together, still on good terms with him, as much as that was possible. The kids stayed with their father; he was the stable one right now. She needed time and space, she knew, but the pain she felt every time she saw them, and then had to say goodbye, sometimes seemed too much to bear. Each time hurt as much as the last. Each time she had to make the decision to leave all over again. Meg wondered if that pain would ever go away.

So here she was, 35 years old, 20 pounds overweight, blue eyes, light brown hair, glasses, no savings, a small monthly check from her husband, no job skills that were usable since she had left professional ministry in the Catholic Church, no longer any religious system left to replace the one she had abandoned, no lover on the horizon, no job prospects—a pretty gloomy picture when she let herself dwell on it.

A lumber truck, passing uncomfortably close, brought her out of her reverie. There was the turn, but she wasn't sure she could find the right parking lot. Since this was a lesbian event, the planners had told the women who were coming not to call attention to themselves by leaving obvious signs of their whereabouts. It was only by chance Meg knew about it. Last week she had overheard a couple of country dykes talking about it at the co-op. There was no way to make this public beach private or safe from possible harassment, so discretion was the password.

Well, it would give her a chance to practice what one woman had called "gaydar," the lesbian equivalent of radar. The more she practiced, the easier it was. When she first identified herself as a lesbian, she'd had no idea how to find others. They had certainly kept themselves well hidden in the past. As she began to learn the signs and signals, she was continually amazed at and thankful for their numbers, and wondered how she had been blind to them before.

She drove her red pickup through the parking areas slowly, her antennae out for clues. This time it wasn't even hard. Not only was there a concentration of women, with a greater number of large dogs than the general population, but their cars gave them away. Bumperstickers made identification easy. "Save Your Mother Earth" and "Eat Organic" proclaimed an old Chevy. "We're Everywhere," the Ford truck next to it stated more boldly. "My Other Car Is A Broom," "I Love the Goddess," and "Born-Again Pagan" plastered an old VW bus. The van next to it declared "Save The Whales" and "You Can't Embrace Your Children With Nuclear Arms." A brave brown Honda next to it fairly shouted out "One In Ten" and "I'm One." Meg laughed, knowing that only a few short months ago she wouldn't have understood the last two. Along with discovery of her sexual orientation was the need for her to learn a whole new language.

Sure she was in the right place, Meg looked for a space for her old Toyota pickup. Since her emergency brake wasn't working, she had to park someplace where the truck wouldn't roll. Her hood latch was broken too, fastened with a piece of baling wire. She pulled in next to a lavender van, the same vintage as hers, also sporting a "One In Ten" sticker, with a body even more dented and beat up than her truck.

She's named her old pickup "Arachne"—spider, spinner, spinster. She had always liked spiders; now they were her totem. They were able to spin their homes out of their bodies and provide for themselves in the web that emerged. That was what she was learning to do.

Now the hard part: getting out and walking into a strange group of women. Meg loved women's gatherings, but she felt so shy and "new" that she had to force herself to be outgoing. She took a deep breath and opened the door, still uncertain of her "lesbian" looks. A beginning "fag tag" straggled down the back of her neck, around which hung a silver image of the Goddess, arms upraised to hold a small lavender amethyst. Usually, she tucked it under her shirt.

To her credit, Meg no longer owned any polyester. Jeans with an elastic waist kept her waist size and weight a secret, even from herself. A turquoise T-shirt proclaimed her as a "Survivor," a rather fitting last present from Kim. Over that, she wore a white turtleneck sweater and an inexpensive navy blue windbreaker. Birkenstocks would have to wait for more income; today, she sported a pair of dingy white tennis shoes. She certainly wasn't a lesbian fashion trend-setter, but with luck, no one would know she had just come out of a 17-year marriage.

As she made her way to the beach, she tried to look friendly but not too eager. Fragments of conversation came to her as she passed by small groups of women, each wrapped up in their own little piece of the world, not noticing the newcomer.

" . . . And then I told her I wasn't interested in just seeing her on occasional weekends. I needed to have a commitment from her . . ." Meg could certainly relate to that.

And a little further, "I discovered this really unique crystal shop. I found an amethyst that I'm making into a necklace. I can feel its power." That started off a whole chain of thoughts. Crystals, psychic healing, smudging with sage, channeling were so alien to her own religious background that she felt lost. There didn't seem to be anything left for her in Christianity except hurt, but she didn't yet know if this strange, new world held anything for her either.

She walked down the beach, each step taking her more surely into lesbian territory, members of the "other world" becoming the unknowing minority. It was odd, as if two worlds were layered on each other, lesbians having special glasses to see both, straights blind to all but their own.

Pausing a moment, she smiled at the odd juxtaposition of two obvious young dykes in baggy cut-offs, white men's tees and vests, one with a purple "fag tag" and the other with the side of her head shaved, strolling hand-in-hand past a middle-aged woman perched uncomfortably on a log, bleached hair peeking out from under a big straw hat, the shine of polyester on her black pants and frilly white blouse. Meg was momentarily blinded by sunlight glancing off the woman's left hand. Some rock! Her own marriage hadn't included anything so pretentious.

Passing several men walking alone, Meg wondered if they noticed how some of the women on the beach were simply ignoring them, saving their greetings for each other. No, she thought, their pride probably made them think that all of the attractive women (according to their standards) were lusting after their bodies. Oh, well, let them have their male vanity. She had better things to do. She had a favorite fantasy involving all lesbians and gays one day putting on purple armbands and wearing them all day—in the workplace, schools, childcare centers, etc. Boy, wouldn't that be an awakening?

Then there were blankets, women, guitars and drums, women, volleyball shouts, women. Strangers. This was it—the gathering she'd come for—but she needed all her willpower not to bolt. "Well, I'm here, right?" she mumbled to herself. "I might as well give myself a chance."

Down at the edge of the water, she saw an outcropping of rock, an old lava bed. Giving herself a breather, she ambled casually over and began a diligent search for marine life. Not much here, just a few mussels and sea anemones.

Unable to resist the delicately swaying tentacles of the anemones, she knelt down in the salt water, warm from the afternoon sun. Gently touching the center of the closest anemone, she forgot herself as it squirted water at her, closing around her finger. Somehow, she felt more at ease with these creatures than her own kind, gathered in small kinship groups on the beach. Well, that was all right, she kept telling herself, she had time. Reaching out to touch a particularly beautiful coral anemone, she heard a voice from behind her. "Hi. I see you like anemones, too."

Startled, Meg turned and looked up. The stranger seemed friendly enough, a bit younger, perhaps in her late twenties. She was tall, on the lean side, short blond hair with highlights standing straight up with a boldness Meg envied. Sensing Meg's shyness, the woman kept talking. "I'm Jody. I don't think I've seen you around here before."

"No," Meg admitted. "I just moved to the coast two months ago. I've been pretty much settling in. Do you like to tidepool?"

Jody smiled. "I love it, and it's a good thing I do. I work down at the marine science center. Inter-tidal zones are my specialty."

Meg's childhood longings swept over her like a gentle wave as she brushed her hands dry on her jeans. As a child growing up in southern California, she had been drawn to the sea. In adolescence, she had found a name for her interest—marine biology. In high school, she had even set up a small marine aquarium in the garage for her pet octopus, Oscar. How in the world did she end up majoring in English literature?

A grinning Jody broke into her reverie. "Hey, have I lost you?"

Meg found herself trusting this stranger. It was as if she were meeting her younger self, untouched by the world's heterosexual demands, strong in her own beauty and self-affirmation.

"The tide's going out. Do you want to follow it with me?"

"Sure." Then, as Meg struggled to get up from an awkward position, Jody reached out. "Here, let me give you a hand." The sinews stood out on Jody's tanned forearms as she pulled Meg to her feet. A shock, a tremor passed through Meg, unexpected. She stood, breathless, holding that hand a moment too long.

She could not have said later how long they wandered or at what point Jody, grinning, put her arm around Meg's shoulders as she pointed out the seals and told her about the midwesterner who'd called the center and asked them to rescue the "drowning dog." She could not have said when Jody held out a hand cradling a tiny crab, how their hands touched as the crab skittled into her own. She could not have said who chased whom as they raced or when she had realized Jody's eyes were bluer than the sea and sky together. All she knew was that she never wanted the afternoon to end.

2
Meg Bolts

Two women with hands and pockets full of shells, one with her heart in her throat, trudged reluctantly back toward the gathering, the sunset fading at their heels. At the parking lot, Jody stopped. "Hey, I don't know about you, but I don't want to carry these shells and rocks all the way down the beach and then back again. Why don't we put them in our cars now?"

Meg nodded. "My car's right over there, next to that lavender van."

"Well, it looks like our cars have an affinity for each other, too. I've had that van since college."

After throwing their shells into the cars, they continued back, but the closer they came to the bonfire flickering in the growing darkness, the slower Meg walked. Jody took over. "Come on, Meg, I'll introduce you."

"Hi, Jody. Who's your friend?" a small woman with straight, long brown hair, and a loose-fitting cotton dress of purple and blue, called out to her. She wore a porcupine quill necklace and yoni earrings. Meg had been startled when she had seen her first pair and had a secret desire to have her own, but she was not yet courageous enough. She was pretty sure that no men or straight women would even recognize the beautiful sterling silver pendant with single inset pearl as a woman's labia, but she was not yet ready to find out.

"Oh, hi, Crystal. Crystal Birdsong, Meg . . ."

"Blake. Glad to meet you, Crystal. What a beautiful name. Is it yours?" Whoops. That was a stupid thing to say. Of course, it was hers. Whose else would it be? Realizing her mistake, Meg blushed. Stammering, she tried to continue, "I, uh, I mean, is it a family name?"

Crystal laughed melodically. "Oh, no, I chose it myself. I love crystals, and I've always felt a special connection with birds. My birth name wasn't *me*, so I changed it seven years ago."

Now *there* was a novel thought. Meg had considered taking back her maiden name when she and Mark separated, but that would just push the patriarchy back a generation. What *would* her name be if she could create it herself?

Crystal sat down on a log stretched out along one side of the fire and motioned Meg to follow. Meg settled next to her reluctantly, her eyes following Jody, taking in the muscled, tanned legs, strong back, tender wisps of blond hair along the back of her neck. Meg's cheeks blushed even redder than the sun had turned them when she realized Crystal was following her gaze with a sidelong, questioning smile. Meg had somehow managed to escape her own adolescence, with all of its awkwardness, passion and intensity. Maybe it was time to do it over—right this time.

She tried to relax as the fire warmed her and food was passed around, but still her eyes sought Jody, who had, suddenly and without explanation, disappeared from sight. Where could she have gone? It was getting darker. Would she have left without saying goodbye?

The Meg saw her on the distant horizon, her outline barely distinguishable in the fading light. She was arguing with another woman, who stumbled from time to time as the two of them walked back toward the circle. They seemed to have reached a truce by the time they sat down across from Meg, on the other side of the leaping flames. Meg tried to turn her flushed face back into the shadows, away from the sight of their thighs and hips, pressed together as they wedged themselves into the only space left. She should have known; Jody had a lover.

She had done it again, committed her emotions before she had enough information. Her "teenager" was having a field day. She kept going back over their conversation, wondering if she had shown Jody too obviously that she might be interested in her. Well . . . who cared! She hadn't done anything wrong. She slipped off the log so she could lean against it, crossing her arms across her chest, tilting her head back and concentrating fiercely on the emerging stars.

Next to her, Crystal began rummaging in her large bag, her hands finally emerging triumphantly with packages of tofu dogs and whole-wheat buns. "Meg, I have plenty. Why don't you take a couple."

Meg was ready to say yes when a couple of new women stepped from the now almost black night into the fire's warm glow. Everyone on the far side of the circle shifted to make room, and as the two settled themselves, flickering light and shadow playing across their faces, Meg, with a start, recognized Kim and Cheryl. Instinctively, she pulled back into the darkness to hide her own features. This was too much.

One reason she had moved to the coast was so that she would never accidentally run into Kim, and here she was, showing up unexpectedly where she had no right to be. Meg wished she could stand her own ground, but coming in the wake of finding out Jody had a lover, this was too much. Time to beat a strategic retreat.

Turning to Crystal, Meg whispered, "Ah, sorry, Crystal, I have to get back. It was nice meeting you." Hastily, she grabbed her windbreaker and backed away from the fire, hoping Kim wouldn't spot her.

Meg was panting by the time she got back to the parking lot, glad she had parked under a light. It was dark and chilly, an ocean breeze cutting like a knife through her too-thin jacket. Swinging into the cab, she turned on the heater, then started to back out as fast as she could. She was halfway out of the parking lot before she noticed the cab was leaning suspiciously to the left.

"Oh, hell, that's all I need, a flat tire. Damned if I'm going to wait around for Triple A. I'll change it myself!" She pulled back into the parking space, got out and discovered the left front tire was flat. It wasn't really too surprising. All traces of tread were gone, Meg counting on faith and luck to protect her until she could afford a new tire. "Well," she said out loud, resolution in her voice, "I'll need the maintenance manual for this. Hope the flashlight works."

Soon she had out an old blanket to kneel on, the manual lying in the gravel next to it, along with the jack and tire iron. She found a stone to place under the opposite wheel to keep the truck from slipping. In less than ten minutes, she had the spare mounted and the flat thrown into the back of the pickup. The emergency had made her focus and concentrate on the problem at hand.

Accidentally, the tire bumped into the hood, making it jiggle a bit too much for Meg. "I'd better tighten the wire," Meg mumbled to herself while leaning the flat against the bumper. The flashlight's beam revealed the wire, stuck between the radiator and front of the truck.

That's odd, Meg thought, as she managed to fish it out and rewire the hood shut, I'm usually pretty good about keeping this wire tight.

But the night was turning chilly and the hour late, so she threw the flat into the back and headed out onto the highway. The second she hit the road, she realized all her old feelings for Kim were still there.

The irony of it all was she still wasn't sure if she was more angry with Kim or herself. True, Kim had made her all sorts of promises that last year. She had said Cheryl's drinking was out of hand, and she was leaving, just waiting for the right time. It seemed Cheryl was always either too drunk or too hung over to talk to. God, what a fool she had been! Meg found herself slamming her fist into the steering wheel.

Yet, to be fair, Meg had cooperated. She had told no one, at Kim's request, not wanting to expose Kim's secret. She had called only when she knew Cheryl was at work. She had pretended to be only friends with Kim when they were together in public. She had lost count of the many furtive kisses they had stolen in women's rooms, writing on the stalls their "signature": "Lesbians unite—as often as possible!" She still remembered with shame the night the security guard had caught them necking in a parking lot, Kim remaining silent, leaving Meg to explain their presence.

Blushing, Meg pulled off the road into her driveway. From the very first, she had loved this little house, one of four in a row that had originally been built for migrant laborers. It was run down, part of the porch supports torn out, the concrete landing cracked and unstable. The inside wasn't much better. The linoleum in the kitchen was faded, stained and rolling up along the seams, making walking a little rocky. The bedroom was small and dark, with a window too small to admit much light; the dank bathroom was cramped, and the tub too short to stretch out in. The living room was shabby, with its thrift shop couch and chair. But its floor-to-ceiling windows looking out on the bay, small back porch and large fireplace, more than made up for the rest of the place.

What had sold Meg on it was the rent. In exchange for helping the owner renovate the four cabins and living there as a caretaker, Meg just had to pay for utilities, driftwood being her main source of heat. The free rent went a long way in her new world.

Every morning, Meg would get up at dawn, light a fire, and take a cup of coffee outside to watch the waves and listen to the seagulls. She hoped that if she could just learn to sit there long enough and patiently enough, the peace she so desperately sought would finally come to her.

She had thought she had made a good beginning until tonight, until the feelings about Kim she thought she had gotten over came rushing back in, upsetting her fragile sense of peace. Too tired to light a fire, Meg turned on her electric blanket and tossed and turned for a long time before sleep, her body again missing Kim's touch. If she still felt this stuck in the morning, maybe she needed to get away for a few days and go camping.

She drifted off to sleep and fell immediately into dreaming. She was twelve, tidepooling with her father. Her rolled up peddle-pushers already wet with salt water, old sneakers gripping the coral-covered rocks, light blue T-shirt blending into the slightly darker ocean. In a little cranny protected from the incoming waves, she knelt down, carefully avoiding the clumps of knee-piercing barnacles. Finding a brittle star, she cradled it in the palm of her hand, her voice rising in excitement. "Dad," the near-teenage girl, still with dreams intact, looked up. "I want to be a marine biologist when I grow up." Then before he could reply, a storm came in, waves and darkness overcoming them. But just before the darkness was complete, she caught a glimpse of a face floating over her, the face of Jody when she first saw her on the shore, a face still showing the enthusiasm and joy Meg had lost.

3
Flight to Lost Lake

Morning finally did come. Meg woke up in a cold sweat, a flood of memories of being with Kim borne in with the incoming tide. Habit got her out of bed and into the kitchen, where she made coffee as depression stalked her like an insatiable beast. Too tired to change the night before, she had slept in her "Survivor" T-shirt. Today, Meg wondered if she might be accused of false advertising. No matter how hard she tried, the peace just would not come, her heart filling with the pain of all her partings.

As she passed through the living room, coffee in hand, Meg turned towards the mantel, a picture of her three kids in the center. It was last Christmas's present to her and Mark, one for each of them, a poignant daily reminder of their now separate lives. Taking her coffee to the back porch, Meg found the driest step, still damp from the night dew.

Well, she could either sit around and indulge her self-pity or do something to fight the building depression. It was time to move on. In just a few minutes, she had piled on the couch her sleeping bag and pillow, ice chest, thermos, Coleman stove and flashlight, a couple of changes of clothes and toiletry items, and a bag of food, mostly coffee and breakfast bars, her two staples in an unstable world. At the last minute, she also threw in the journal that recorded page by page, in precise and poignant detail, the last year of her relationship with Kim. She hadn't been able to pick it up since that night in April when Kim told her it was over.

The agony of that night was still imprinted on her heart. She remembered hanging up the phone in shock, Kim's words still ringing in her ears, "I've decided to stay with Cheryl." Shouting "Damn! Damn! No!," she had systematically picked books off the shelves, throwing them in a rage at the brick wall of the den. Finally exhausted, her rage spent, she went to bed, aided by two heavy-duty anti-depressants. For days, she stayed drugged, afraid to trust herself again to the capricious cruelties of her life. Each time she was forced to consciousness, she felt the pain anew, the pain of losing the woman she had given her heart and body to. It felt as if an arbitrary and cruel god had come down to rip her heart from her chest. Days later, when she had come out of her stupor, her chest hurt as if her heart really had been removed by force.

The sense of betrayal and loss still made it hard at times to remember anything good about the relationship. Now, though, she thought back to a weekend last October when the two of them had gone camping in the mountains, something she hadn't done since childhood. Emotionally, the trip had been frustrating; Kim was still finding reasons not to tell Cheryl. In many ways that trip represented all the pain of their relationship. But it had also polished Meg's old camping skills. Now was the time to meet her demons head on by going back to the scene of that horrible weekend. Maybe there she could find the secret that would free her to live her new life.

As she got in the truck, she remembered last night's flat. There was no way she would dare those backroads without a spare. Swinging by the Texaco station, she dropped off her flat to be repaired and borrowed a retread as a spare. If only she could afford four new steel-belted radials. But her alimony was stretched as far as it would go. There weren't many jobs on the coast, and she'd probably end up cleaning motel rooms. She just wasn't ready yet. Maybe if she could face her demons in the forest, she would be able to face the dragons of the workplace.

As she drew near Mt. Hood, her muscles gradually relaxed. It was Monday morning, and the traffic was light; she felt like she was playing hooky. The sun began to warm the inside of the cab, the breeze from the half-open window rushing across her face. The orchards on both sides of the road were loaded with ripening cherries, the pear and apple trees still blossoming. It was almost impossible to stay depressed about the little deaths in her life when the surrounding fields were proclaiming that life, when given the chance, would always come back in abundance.

With the least bit of luck and the detailed forest service map left over from her last adventure, she could find the same site they had camped in last time, next to Lost Lake. Even at the time of her trip with Kim she had reflected on the irony of the name. She had certainly felt lost then, as she did now. But it was time she found herself.

Meg's luck held as she pulled into a campsite. Fortunately, she had remembered to fill up a five-gallon can of water for drinking and washing. It didn't take her long to set up camp, since she planned on sleeping in the truck.

Pouring that last cup of coffee from her thermos, Meg picked up her journal and searched for the tree she had found the last time. She sat again at its trunk, leaning into it, and opened her journal to the date she was looking for, October 12. Afraid of what she might find but needing to face it head-on, she read:

"It would be a good day to die today. I am so damn tired of fighting all the time. I found a beautiful tree that looks on the hills surrounding Lost Lake. I wanted to wrap myself up in a sleeping bag, sit there from dawn to dusk, and then put a bullet through my brain. I was doing fine until this morning."

God, it sounded so adolescent, so serious, so melodramatic. At that point, Meg remembered trudging to the van and taking the bullets out of the .32. It would have been too tempting to use them. She had tried to tell Kim how much it hurt her each time Kim denied that they were lovers, each time Kim promised to tell Cheryl, then found another excuse to delay. By that October weekend, Meg had already lost whatever self-respect she had, but still couldn't let go of the crumbs she got from Kim's table. She was so afraid of being without Kim that she kept believing her promises and supporting her in her deceit.

The whole weekend had been one of push and pull—increasing closeness, then the lie of their furtive relationship shoving them apart again. Their departure had been especially painful. Kim had not told Cheryl that she was going camping with Meg, but by herself. Instead of Kim using her one-person tent, the two of them had used Meg's larger one. Yet right before they finished packing, Kim took a new tarp rope out of its package and dragged it through the dirt. It took Meg only a moment to figure out what she was doing, making the rope look used so Kim could continue lying to Cheryl. It made Meg sad and sick to her stomach to see a 45-year-old woman acting like a child, trying to hide a spot in the carpet from her mother by moving a chair over it. Why couldn't Meg then see her *own* cowardice, her fear of standing up to Kim and saying, "No more lies?"

Sadness engulfed Meg as she read the journal. There was still a huge vacant space that had been filled with her love for Kim, but she was beginning to get some perspective. Some day in the future—perhaps not so distant as she had first imagined—she would be able to read the whole thing through and laugh at the intensity of her first lesbian love.

One last entry for old times' sake: July 6, two days after Meg and Kim first made love, on their way to the Bay Area for a two-week course in body-centered spirituality.

How can I find the words to express what has happened to me the last three days? I slept fairly well Thursday night, then got to Kim's around 7:20 a.m. The day went well—lots of time to look at each other and touch and be more comfortable with our growing intimacy. We got to a small town 15 miles north of Redding around 4:30 and found a room at the El Rancho Motel. It was truly a blessed and holy night. Kim wanted to know how I had fantasized this—I said first to shower, then be made love to, then learn to love her. So, we did. It felt so good and peaceful and right and natural. When she stroked my breasts and licked and suckled them, it was obviously very sexual, but even more my coming to know the sacredness of my own body. She touched my vulva with such softness and reverence and honor, with her fingers seeking out my innermost places that I had always kept hidden and protected, and my clitoris rejoicing in no longer having to withhold its joy from the knowledge of others.

I kissed her, then—finally—was able to fondle her breasts and stroke them and and lick them and suck her nipples—coming home at last. I found her with my fingers, and her coming to climax with my fingers inside her was as if I were there with my whole being. She opened to me and responded to me wholly and without reservation. Waves and waves of fluid, wet muscle surrounded and compressed my fingers. It was the first time I had any idea of the power and depth of female sexuality.

Later, after sleeping, she made love to me again; I masturbated with her fingers inside me and her body next to me. It was so hard to do—to tell her how I reach orgasm, realizing that I probably couldn't be that way with her. Yet I could allow her to be present with me as I became more and more sexually aroused. I didn't need to be frustrated, withdrawn or angry when I didn't come. That was a real gift of vulnerability and of special intimacy I gave her.

Meg didn't know whether to laugh or cry. Part of her could see the overdramatization, but she could still feel the joy of first discovery and the uncertainty which caused her to question whether she would have the same intense feelings with another lover—indeed, if she would ever have another lover.

But enough was enough. She set the journal aside and decided just to enjoy herself. She had food, some good books, spectacular scenery and her own company for the next few days. It was time for *her*. Throwing the remains of the coffee into the dirt, she stretched, then walked down to the lake, book in hand, a spring in her step for the first time in months. She found a soft mound of grass next to the shore, took off her shoes and socks and put her feet into the slightly chill water. Breathing in the crisp mountain air, she opened the book, settled back and began: "It was a soft spring day on the moors. Catherine Harding waited expectantly for her friend, Laney Carl, to show up . . ."

So immersed was she in the book, Meg didn't notice the air growing chill and the summer sun beginning to set, sending its rays across the now rippling lake. Only when it became too dark to read did she look up, regretful, surprised that the day had gone so pleasantly and rapidly. Standing up and stretching, Meg murmured to the spirits of the lake, " Maybe I'm going to make it after all." With that declaration coming from deep within her, she walked back to the campsite, ready for a companionable evening with herself by a campfire.

4
Tragedy Strikes

The joy of breakfast bars was dimming; her socks were thick with sweat, dust, and dried bits of mid-summer leaves. Still, Meg had managed five nights in the wilderness by herself—no small feat for someone whose last trip to Girl Scout camp was the summer of 1963. Halfway back to the coast, her desire for hot food, cooked by someone else, overcame her need to rush home for a long, hot bath. She pulled over at a truck stop, choosing a solitary booth to hide her somewhat disheveled appearance and unquestionably gamey smell.

After two hamburgers, large fries, blueberry pie a 'la mode and a large Dr. Pepper, Meg was ready to finish her homeward journey. It was tempting to call her kids—she hadn't talked to them in over a week—and even more tempting to turn off the highway towards their home for a quick visit, but she was learning it was not always wise to try to fill up her loneliness. Much better to wait a couple of days, fight it out herself, then give them a call.

In the late dusk, tired out but satisfied with herself, Meg pulled up in front of her cabin, a place she was beginning to call home. After starting the fire, glancing through the mail and pouring herself her traditional diet Dr. Pepper, she settled into a deep, hot bath with a paperback detective novel she wasn't afraid of getting wet. Subsequent to days of sponge baths with lukewarm water in limited supply, she found the annoyingly short bathtub luxurious by comparison.

Two hours and two shampoos later, Meg emerged feeling refreshed and clean for the first time in days. Wrapping herself in her old terrycloth robe, soft and sweet-smelling, she replenished her drink and stretched out on the saggy sofa, a delicious change after sleeping on a thin foam pad in the back of her truck. She rummaged through the mail she had thrown on the coffee table when she had come in. The ads weren't even worth opening; she tossed them, crumpled, into the fireplace. On to the papers. She might as well begin with the local paper, published only once a week. Maybe something interesting was happening in town, although she doubted it.

Usually the headlines were something like "Salmon Season Opens" or "City Raises Water Rates," but this issue was different. In the middle of the front page was a picture of a van being hoisted out of the bay. Although the picture was black-and-white, the van looked strangely familiar. Meg put on her glasses and drew the paper closer. It was Jody's van. Her jaw tightened and her stomach churned as she started reading.

"Van Plunges Into Bay; Passenger Dies."

"Early Sunday morning, a van carrying two women plunged into the bay. The passenger in the vehicle was drowned; the driver managed to escape through the window. She stopped a passing car whose occupants tried unsuccessfully to rescue the other woman. The body was recovered late Sunday afternoon with the help of the state police.

"The survivor was taken to the hospital, where she was released following examination by emergency room personnel. Several open containers of beer were found on the floorboard of the van, but it has not yet been determined if alcohol was a contributing cause in the accident.

"The county medical examiner is due to release the results of the autopsy later this week. The vehicle has been impounded by the state police to check for mechanical failure. The attorney for the city of Newbridge has asked for a full investigation in hopes of forestalling a lawsuit against the city for what critics have called an unsafe parking situation.

"No charges have yet been filed, pending the completion of the investigation. Names of the victim and her companion have not been released, pending notification of next of kin."

Meg had thought she had used up her quota of emotions for at least a month on her camping trip, but she was wrong. She could feel her pulse begin to race, a shock run through her body, a clutching in her chest. "I hope it wasn't Jody who drowned," she heard herself saying out loud. Then guilt hit. She didn't even know the other woman, and now she was wishing her dead. Well, no, it was just that she wished Jody alive. She didn't think it was quite the same thing.

There was no way Meg could stand the suspense of waiting five more days until the next paper. Who did she know who would know which one of the women had drowned? Frantically, she searched her memory for clues to last Saturday afternoon, whcih now seemed an eternity ago. Her problems paled in the face of this tragic and senseless sudden death.

"Crystal!" Of course, she remembered now. Crystal Birdsong was such an usual name she would be easy to find—assuming, of course, that she believed in telephones and her number was listed.

Meg grabbed the local phone directory and looked up the city of Newbridge. She remembered that Crystal said she had lived just down the coast from the beach. No luck. "Calm down," she kept repeating to herself. "Maybe the operator would know." Hands still shaking, Meg managed to dial information. There it was, a new listing. Good.

Taking several deep breaths to center herself, Meg picked up the phone again to call. It was late, after eleven, but this was not a time to stand on politeness. The phone rang six times, and Meg was about to hang up when someone picked up the receiver.

"Hello?" a sleepy voice mumbled.

Oh, no, Meg almost said aloud. She had awakened someone she hardly knew. Oh, well, it was important. She forged ahead. "Hi, is this Crystal?"

"Who is this? What time is it anyway?"

"I'm sorry to wake you, Crystal. It's about eleven, and I know it's late, but it's important. Oh, this is Meg. I met you last weekend at the women's gathering. I've been out of town camping, and I just read the paper . . . the van accident. That was Jody's van, wasn't it?"

"Yeah . . . It's really unbelievable, isn't it?" Crystal spoke with real feeling.

Meg's voice stumbled with awkwardness and discomfort. "Ah, I, uh, don't know how to ask this, but who drowned?"

"It was Susan."

Thank God, Meg thought, as a barely audible sigh of relief escaped. "Was that Jody's lover?"

"Uh-huh. Jody always drove, especially since Susan started drinking again last year. That's why they were fighting at the gathering."

That explained the stumbling Meg had witnessed. "How's Jody taking it?"

"Not too well. She's pretty much shut herself up in her house, and she's keeping to herself. Her friends are doing all we can . . . but Jody closes up when she's hurting."

"Well, I know it's late," said Meg. "Thanks for telling me. I'm so sorry . . ."

"Me, too. It puts everything else in perspective, doesn't it? Let's get together soon and talk. I seem to remember I owe you a tofu hot dog."

Meg laughed in spite of herself. "Thanks, Crystal. I'll call soon. Sorry I woke you up."

As Meg hung up, she was almost happy. She did not have to grieve for Jody after all. She wanted so much to pick up the phone again and call her, but she restrained herself. If Jody was closed down to friends, how would she react to Meg, practically a stranger? Silently, passionately, she sent a blessing. Perhaps someday their lives would touch again.

5
To Be (Out) Or Not To Be: That Is The Question

Meg woke feeling drugged. Looking around the room, she wondered where she was. It was too dark to see more than dim outlines, but the sound of the surf reassured her that she was home. Then memories of the tragedy flooded in. She tossed off the covers, flinging them to the floor. Her mind began where it had left off the night before, flashing vivid images of Jody, in pain, alone, unreachable.

After nearly an hour of anguish, Meg let the sunlight flooding her window release her. She had enough problems she *could* deal with, even if she didn't particularly want to. Alimony wasn't leaving her enough for emergencies, let alone fun. Her meager savings had disappeared in conjuring up the sparse furnishings of her home. If she didn't do something to add to her income, she wouldn't ever be able to pick up her tire at the garage, not to mention fixing her broken hood latch and emergency brake.

This was as good a day as any to start job-hunting. Stoking the fire and pouring herself a fresh cup of coffee, Meg walked out to her back porch, local paper in hand. Leaning against the side of the house, her feet resting on the step below, she turned to the "Help Wanted" section before her resolve could fade.

"Fabricators and millwrights." No. Meg put an X through that. "Carpenters and laborers." No. Good enough for rough carpentry and stop-gap repairs, but that was it. Another X.

Tourist industry and nursing home jobs? None of them sounded too cheery. "Dishwasher, busperson, bartender." No. Counter work at Dairy Queen? Meg shuddered.

Well, only a couple more left. "Hospitality aides needed. Provide assistance with daily living skills for elderly. $3.50 an hour. Full or part time." No thanks. She had been a chaplain on a geriatric ward in a state mental hospital a couple of years before and had no desire to provide physical care.

"Motel maid, weekend relief. Hourly wages. Apply in person, Mermaid Hotel." It seemed to be the best of a bad lot. At least, she wouldn't have to work directly with people, and two days a week was probably all she could take.

If she was going to do it, now was the time, before her nerve left. At least, she wouldn't have to dress up. A nicer pair of jeans and her light blue knit sweater would do. Earrings would distract the manager from her dyke haircut and give a more feminine look. But her shoes were a wreck after hiking through the woods for a week. It was time for a new pair.

After changing into her job-hunting outfit, Meg drove to the shopping mall with ten dollars in her pocket for shoes. As she pulled into the parking lot, she noticed a table outside the main entrance, an older woman behind it. Meg hoped to slip by without being noticed. No such luck.

"Excuse me, I have a petition here. Would you be interested in signing it?"

She was caught. "What's it about?"

The woman straightened her shoulders and raised her chin. "I'm a member of Citizens Concerned about Morality. We're working to overthrow the governor's executive order. He wants to make it legal for homosexuals to have special job protections that heterosexuals don't have. He's just trying to make homosexuality an acceptable lifestyle, and we all know it isn't. We have to stop him now before homosexuals demand all sorts of rights, as if they were just like us."

Her face shocked into an impassive mask, Meg boiled inside. Afraid of losing control, she turned away with a polite, "No, thanks, I'm not interested," and sought sanctuary in the store, breathing again only when the electric doors closed behind her.

"Damn it, Blake, don't you have any guts at all?" she berated herself. "Why couldn't you tell the old bitch to bug off? What right does she have to judge anyone or look at me disapprovingly? Tell me I'm a sinner or that I'm going to hell? If you don't speak out, how can you expect anyone else to?"

But she wasn't ready for the kind of confrontation. It was going to take her a long time to decide how and where to be "out." She had heard enough horror stories about what happened to lesbians to make her cautious.

But that didn't make her any less angry with herself. On her way to the shoe department, she bumped into a rack of purses and knocked them to the floor, letting out a "Damn!" She made a fumbling attempt to pick them up before ducking down a side aisle. After finding the shoes, she grabbed the first pair that fit. On her way out, she checked the door for more petitioners and, the coast temporarily clear, sneaked out to her truck, all the while berating herself for her cowardice.

Sitting in the cab of the truck, Meg took some time to calm down. Finally, she put on her new shoes and drove by the Mermaid Hotel to get a feel for it. Turning left at the light, she could see down to the beach. There it was. She circled the block several times, checking it out. She was relieved to see that it had only ten or twelve units. The building itself was a little shabby but essentially in good condition. At least, it wasn't one of those gigantic chains.

"Okay, Blake. What's the big deal? At worst, they can say no, and then you can take the rest of the day off. Let's go," she said to herself.

After parking, she found the manager's office. No one was in, so she took a deep breath and rang the bell on the counter. The door behind the counter opened, and a small, grey-haired woman in light blue, polyester pants and a floral blouse came in. "Can I help you?"

"I hope so. I'm interested in the position I saw advertised in the paper."

The woman smiled warmly, her blue eyes sparkling behind her glasses. "Have you ever done this kind of work before?"

"No," Meg began slowly. "But I ran a household for a number of years, and I'm sure I can do the work."

Almost apologetically, the woman said, "The pay is just $3.50 an hour, with no benefits."

Meg smiled back, sensing the job was hers for the asking. "That's okay. I just need a part-time job right now."

"Oh, that's wonderful! Can you start today? Sally can show you what to do. She has a couple more rooms to get ready today. Oh, my name is Mrs. Laetitia Green."

"That's fine. My name is Meg Blake."

Feeling quite virtuous, Meg followed Mrs. Green to cabin 11, trying on the title "motel maid," as she walked.

Mrs. Green pushed on the partially opened door. As she did, a woman of about 30, weraing jeans and an old sweatshirt, her long brown hair held back by a rubber band, came out of the bathroom carrying the overflowing trash can.

"Sally, meet Meg. I just hired her as relief help. Can you show her the ropes?"

"Sure. I can use some help. Since Carol quit last Tuesday, I've been doing all the work myself. Welcome aboard."

"Well, I'll leave you two to it. When you're done here, come to the office, have some iced tea, and we'll complete the paperwork." With that, Mrs. Green turned, leaving Meg to Sally's instruction.

It turned out not to be that hard to learn the job. Sally was a thorough teacher and had a lot of time-saving techniques worked out. She also seemed a pleasant enough companion, but it was hard for Meg to keep up with her non-stop chatter. Soon she found out that an occasional grunt or "Oh, yeah?" was enough response, leaving her mind free for other things.

However, her attention was abruptly drawn back to the present. Emptying ashtrays, Sally said, "Did you hear about that van accident last week? It probably wasn't an accident."

"What?"

"Yeah. My boyfriend's a reserve police officer, and he said that the case is still open and that detectives had impounded the van. He says people are saying those two women were, ah, you know . . .," Sally paused uncomfortably, "lovers. I just don't understand that, if you can have a man. I don't know any women like that. How about you?"

Oh, hell, not again, twice in the same day! Meg managed a noncomittal noise, hoping Sally wouldn't notice. It seemed to work; her co-worker began another thread of her non-stop monologue.

Meg retreated inward again. Wasn't it enough that Susan had died? Now this! She was sure that there would be no substance to these rumors, but she was beginning to realize that being labeled lesbian wasn't going to be any easier here than in the city. Someday—soon—she was going to have to make a decision about whether to take the risk of being "out."

Somehow, Meg managed to get through her first day as a maid, filled out the paperwork and got herself home. It was time for another long, hot bath, perhaps a walk on the beach, and a steak, baked potato, salad and detective novel. Tomorrow would come soon enough, but she had certainly had her fill of today.

6
A Night On The Town

The next few weeks didn't go too badly. Meg showed up to work at seven Saturday and Sunday mornings and worked hard until she was finished, usually two or three in the afternoon. To reward herself for her diligence, she gave herself the remainder of the days off, renting a movie on Saturday nights and finishing Sundays with a new detective story.

Monday through Friday she would write or work on renovating the cabins. After finishing the inside painting, Meg worked on the outside whenever the weather permitted. Mornings were usually chilly and overcast, but the long summer evenings allowed her to work as long as she wanted. The grey with bright blue trim looked solid with just a touch of sassiness.

Then there were Wednesdays—"Family Night." Dutifully, Meg would drive the 45 miles to visit her kids, knowing. even before she left her cabin, that the time would be too short for the intimacy they all needed. The youngest, Stacey, would be standing impatiently on the porch if it wasn't raining, or just inside the door if it was, waiting to fling herself into Meg's arms. Tom would be barricaded in his room with his TV tuned in to Oprah Winfrey or Phil Donahue. Alyson, the oldest, equally afraid of being quiet or alone, would be in the midst of a flurry of activity she had created.

The four of them would all spend the evening sitting around the dinner table, long after the dishes were cleared, talking, playing games, or doing homework. The activity itself didn't really matter; it was their way of being together, trying to absorb enough of one another's presence to last the coming week. The time would go by so fast, no matter how hard Meg tried to hang on to it, and all too soon she would be saying goodbye and driving home in the dark—to an empty house.

This routine went on for weeks without interruption or variation. Ever since her camping trip just after the women's gathering, no one had called Meg, no events that she knew about had happened in the women's community. It was as if it had folded up into itself like a threatened sea anemone, awaiting friendlier tides.

It wasn't surprising that Meg lit into the *Clothes Closet* one Saturday afternoon in early August after an especially long day at the motel. Meg dragged herself back to the cabin to find the paper nestled among her bills. Excited, she poured herself a Dr. Pepper and took the paper to the back porch. The faded cedar boards still held the heat from the afternoon sun, warming Meg's back as she leaned against them.

The headlines caught her eye: "Anti-Gay Initiative Gains Momentum." Rapidly skimming the article, she read the introduction. "No state official shall forbid the taking of any personnel action against any state employee based on the sexual orientation of such employee." It was worse than she had thought. How could the Citizens Concerned for Morality claim they were only trying to keep homosexuals from being a protected group? This went much further than that, making witch hunts a protected activity.

Furious, Meg hit the step with her fist, "Damn, damn, damn! Self-righteous prigs! What do they want—a theocracy?" Taking several deep breaths, Meg turned the page, not wanting to deal with God's hit squad any more. The August sun was still warm, the winds playful, the tide continuing to flow in, all oblivious to the foibles of human nature.

The headline on page two was no better: "Clinic Protestors Continue to Harrass Clients and Staff." Were these self-righteous bigots everywhere? Startled at the vehemence of her reaction, Meg put the paper down. How odd it was that she had grown up so violently opposed to abortion, and now she was just as surely for a woman's right to choose.

Born and raised Episcopalian, Meg had thrived in an all-girls Catholic high school. She had particularly delighted in the stories of the saints, one of her favorites being Maria Goretti, a young Italian girl who fought so hard to keep from being raped that her attacker killed her. Years later, repenting, he went on to become a Franciscan priest. It was just assumed that, if a girl did survive a rape and get pregnant, the noble and godly thing to do would be to have the child.

Meg wondered how she could have been so naive. She was in her late twenties before anything had made her question the underlying patriarchal values of her life. First had come her work at the women's shelter. Ironically, she had still been pro-life at first, until she saw up-close the male violence and coercion that had dictated the terms of these women's lives. She remembered the first day she had gone to the shelter as a volunteer; a woman sitting on the front couch jumped in fear when Meg walked in. She recalled with particular pain holding a one-year-old little girl, who had been born to a violently abusive father. As Meg rocked her, the crying child finally gave into exhaustion, but even in her sleep her hands and feet were clenched, as if holding her body in readiness for the next shout or blow.

The next spring, Meg and Mark had found out that their youngest, Stacey, had been sexually molested by the school janitor. There had been an investigation by the sheriff's office and Children's Services Division, testifying in front of the grand jury, and the trial itself. Yes, the man had been convicted and sent to the county jail for six months, but his actions had changed their family forever. For almost a year afterward, it was all Stacey could talk about. The family had gone into therapy, and Stacey went by herself once a week. Meg had lost count of the times Stacey had come to her needing reassurance, usually beginning with "Mommy, tell me about the time you were molested." Then Meg would tell her about Mr. Hicks, the man who had lived across the street when she was a child, the one who had kissed her lasciviously on the lips after she had come to trust him as a grandfather. Meg had fled, never to return, keeping the memories a secret until her own daughter was molested. That was the only story that gave Stacey any comfort.

Stacey's schoolwork had fallen off; she'd had nightmares, had been preoccupied with the incident, and had withdrawn from friends. Meg had been very grateful that the janitor hadn't actually raped her. But what if Stacey had been older, what if she had gotten pregnant? How dare anyone outside their family dictate that they had to go through that unwanted pregnancy! How dare anyone try to get a constitutional amendment to protect the eggs fertilized by a man's act of violence against a woman!

By then, Meg was breathing rapidly, face flushed, jaw tight. Time for a break. Standing up, she hoisted the axe next to the steps and began to split wood, going as fast and hard as she could. "Take that, you fucking bastards!" she cried out on her first swing. "How does that feel, you self-righteous witchhunters!" got her through the second. As the pile of split logs grew beside her, her anger diminished, and Meg, exhausted and sweating, returned to the paper, having at least temporarily "exorcised" her demons.

No longer in the mood for news, Meg turned to the entertainment page. Lots of good movies, but the distance to Portland was a long way to drive just for a movie. Then she saw a picture of Cris Williamson, with the caption, "Cris in town for Sunday concert." That was more like it. Payday wasn't until the end of the month, but Meg still had twenty-three dollars left. It would be tight, but she could just afford a ticket and cheap dinner and even lunch the next day if she could find a place to sleep for free. It had been a long time since she had slept in Portland, but she did have one name in her book—Geri, who owned her own futon company and had lots of space and plenty of beds. Kim and she had stayed there one night, and it had seemed like there had always been women going in and out. Well, the worst she could do was say no. It was worth a try.

Getting up from the porch, Meg went inside to call. The phone rang several times before someone picked it up.

"Hello?"

"Hi, Geri. This is Meg Blake. I don't know if you remember me. I stayed at your place once with Kim."

"Oh, sure. I remember you. Didn't you move to the coast after you and Kim broke up?"

"I'm calling from there now. Is there any chance you could put me up next Sunday night? I want to go hear Cris Williamson, and I need a place to crash."

"Sure. No problem. There'll be a lot of women from out of town staying here . . . but we can always squeeze in one more. Just bring a sleeping bag. You know where the key is."

"Thanks, Geri. I really need a break. I'll see you next week."

As she hung up, Meg was quite pleased with herself. It had been hard for her to ask people for favors. She could hardly wait for next weekend. It was time to go back into the city and be in the midst of women again—if only for a short time.

7
Conflicts

All week Meg waited anxiously for her night on the town. It had been months since she had been to the city. As the weekend drew near, she washed and ironed clothes, packed her bags and gassed up the truck. It was hard focusing on work the Sunday of the concert, so she worked very fast, knowing she could leave as soon as the last room was cleaned.

Finishing almost an hour early, Meg rushed home. A quick shower and change into her concert clothes and she was on 101 north. Ordinarily, she loved driving. She would put on a tape of Meg Christian, Cris Williamson or Holly Near, roll down the window and put the radio on full volume. But today was different. She had forgotten about the tourists' weekly migratory patterns. Friday evenings it was bumper to bumper from the city to the coast and now, Sunday afternoon, they were lined up, motorhomes clogging the one-lane highway, trying to get back to the city for Monday morning jobs. It took all her patience to keep herself from blindly pulling around some of the more lethargic beasts.

It was almost seven before she took the city center exit and tried to find the concert hall. Having managed to misplace her city map, Meg tried to find the place by memory but got tangled up in the maze of one-way streets and bus-only lanes without spotting it. By the time she decided to find a phone booth and pinpoint the exact address, Meg was in an older residential section of the city, in a beautiful, well-kept neighborhood, with single-family Victorians mixed in with a few apartments. Trees lined the streets, and late-summer roses, still in full bloom, nestled next to the houses, like fledglings crowding around their mother. It was easy to see why Portland was called "The City of the Roses."

Turning a corner, still looking for a phone booth, she was suddenly shocked out of her reverie. There in front of her was an office building spray-painted with blood-red, angry graffiti.

"Baby killers!" said one, another "Murderers!" Slowing down, she saw the sign out front, "Family Planning Clinic." The violence the slogans threatened seemed so out of place here. This must be where the pro-life people were focusing their demonstrations against legal abortions.

She wished she could make these bigots spend a day at a women's shelter, up close to the individual faces that were victims of male pain and violence, but she knew it wouldn't do any good. Pious platitudes could always overpower common sense and reality. Never again would she herself support the premise that made any woman's womb captive and her body a prison, with male violence the assailant and men's secular and religious laws the enforcers. Maybe it was time to start fighting these theocrats with more than thoughts . . .

But it was getting late. After spotting a phone booth, Meg pulled up and found the address of the concert hall. Within minutes, she was back downtown, on the right street this time. As she drew closer to the auditorium, she knew she was no longer lost. The streets were filled with women, some driving by, honking and waving, others already on foot. Women calling out to one another, their energy mounting. Where had they been when Meg was growing up, lonely and feeling like she just didn't fit in the only world she knew?

After she found a parking space, Meg joined the throng of women, being carried along with them almost without volition, as the stream flowed into the concert hall. She had just settled herself in an aisle seat when the lights dimmed and the crowd grew hushed.

It didn't take long for the magic to work its spell. Meg didn't fight it, sinking deeply into her seat and letting the music wash over her and cleanse her, washing away her loneliness, her uncertainty about her future, and most importantly, her guilt over leaving her children. It seemed only moments before intermission. Slowly and reluctantly, Meg stood up to stretch. As she stepped into the aisle, she collided suddenly with a woman hurrying up to the lobby. Turning around, Meg cried out, "Mary!"

"Meg!" The woman, tall, angular, in her mid-thirties and dressed like a clothes-conscious butch, hugged Meg. "I haven't seen you in months! How are you doing?"

Mary certainly had a right to know. The day after Kim had dumped her, Meg, still in shock and near despair, had called Mary. Afraid that Meg was suicidal, Mary had called Meg's therapist. The two of them convinced her to go to Mary's house, where Meg, with the help of a sleeping pill, had slept the afternoon away in restless dreams.

"Getting by. I'm getting settled at the coast, but I really miss my old friends. This is the first time I've ventured into town since Kim dumped me." Usually, Meg was more guarded, but she owed Mary a deeper kind of truth. They had known each other for years, working together in the Catholic Church and coming out together. They had never become lovers but had supported each other as they took short flights into their new world as baby dykes.

"Why don't you come over to the P.D. afterwards, and we can catch up on each other?"

"Sounds good, Mary. Why don't we meet in the lobby afterwards, and we can drive over together? Their parking lot is going to be jammed."

As she returned to her seat, Meg remembered the time Mary had called her in as a last-minute replacement for what was to have been Mary's trip to the coast with her first potential lover. The two of them had lain in the big double bed together, sharing their still unfulfilled fantasies about their first lesbian love affair. Well, that time had come and gone for both of them, more painful and joyous than either had then been capable of imagining.

Still a couple of minutes to curtain time, Meg looked over the audience to see if she could spot any more acquaintances. Suddenly, she felt as if someone had punched her in the stomach. There, down front on the right, she saw Kim, her head nestled on Cheryl's shoulder. A shaft of jealousy pierced her, followed closely by betrayal. "Damn it!" Meg muttered out loud. "That should be me there, with her head on my shoulder!" Then the tears began to come, pushing their way insistently through her tightly closed lids. Fortunately, the lights dimmed, leaving Meg in the forgiving darkness.

Somehow, she managed to get through the rest of the concert, although memories of her first love kept grabbing her and shaking her violently in their teeth. Where the hell had all that emotion come from? Hadn't she broken the power of the beasts in her camping trip? Why were they still holding her in their jaws? Maybe running into Mary had brought back some fresh memories that now had to be laid to rest.

Cris left the stage, but the crowd was unwilling to let her go so easily, their applause bringing her back for an encore. With a sole spotlight on her, the rest of the stage in darkness, Cris began what had been Kim and Meg's song, "Lullaby."

> "Like a ship in the harbor,
> Like a mother and child,
> Like a light in the darkness,
> I'll hold you a while."

The tears sprang loose again, Meg remembering how they had held each other closely and lovingly whenever they had heard this song, resting in each other's arms, believing their love would grow stronger until they could live with each other openly and proudly. She still didn't know what had happened. Was all of it a lie? Would she ever be able to trust herself to another woman's arms again? The tears continued, drenching her shirt. The woman to Meg's left, a total stranger, sensing Meg's pain, put her arm around Meg while she continued to cry.

The song continued,

> "We'll rock on the water,
> I'll cradle you deep,
> And hold you while angels
> Sing you to sleep."

What a laugh! Kim no longer held her, despite her promises, and Meg hadn't encountered any angels willing to take over the job. Maybe she would just have to rock herself to sleep for the rest of her life. She didn't see any likely replacements on the horizon, and her self-confidence was still at an all-time low.

But the music kept coming. Soon the whole room was full of women singing the lullaby, over and over again, their voices building in strength and beauty as they sang. Finally, much to her surprise, Meg heard her own voice join the others, faltering at first, then growing in conviction as she sang the words she thought she no longer believed. Maybe everything would be all right. The world was full of women, and she would find another who was more deserving of her trust. In the meantime, she had herself, and she was beginning to realize that that was no small gift.

8
Night in a Futon Factory

Meg left the concert hall as quickly as she could, and found her truck. The lullaby had soothed her so much that the thought of going to a crowded bar was jarring. Besides, Kim might be there, and she just wasn't in the mood to meet her face to face. She would call Mary the next day and give her apologies. Still, she wasn't quite ready to turn in, so she drove around the darkened streets, enjoying the full moon and warm summer air, laden with the scent of blossoms.

Suddenly, Meg noticed it was almost midnight. Realizing how tired she was, she drove to the futon shop, along streets now virtually deserted. The shop was in a half-residential, half-business neighborhood, right next to a convenience store, thus assuring it a wide variety of passersby. After finding a parking place right out front, Meg grabbed her sleeping bag and pillow and started up the unlit stairs. As her eyes adjusted to the darkness, she saw a form draped over the third step. Getting closer, she realized it was the sleeping body of a youngish man, brown paper bag on the step below him. So as not to disturb him, more for her sake than his, she gingerly stepped over his body, glad that he kept sleeping. Coming from a small rural town had just not prepared her to handle drunks and panhandlers.

The front door was still unlocked, even at this time of night. Meg dropped her sleeping bag at her feet, pulled the door firmly closed and slid the deadbolt into place. Hearing sounds from the kitchen, she followed the voices, hoping to find Geri home. Several women were gathered around the stove, talking all at once and stirring up a suspiciously vegetarian-looking concoction. Four faces, none of them Geri's, turned to her.

"Hi, I'm Meg. Geri said I could crash her tonight. Is she home?"

The woman closest to her responded. "Hi, Meg. No, she isn't back yet. I'm Pat, and this is Linda, and that's Wanda and that's Trish."

"Glad to meet you. Do you know where I can spread out my sleeping bag?"

Pat paused a moment. "All the upstairs rooms are taken. Geri told me I could crash on one of the futons in the shop. There's another one in there that you could use."

"Thanks," Meg smiled. "That sounds like a real adventure."

She was turning to leave when Wanda called her back. "There's plenty here. Why don't you join us?"

"As long as I'm not intruding."

"Don't be silly."

The invitation sounded sincere, and Meg was hungry. "Sure, I'd love to. What are you making?"

"Just a stir-fry. Tofu . . . rice . . . you know . . ." Meg tried not to wince. Well, it wasn't hamburgers, but she could always sneak out to the mini-market next door for Hostess cupcakes if it were inedible. The meal was ready in a matter of minutes and, food and the inevitable herb tea in hand, the five of them crowded into the dining area. There was barely enough room to walk, since the boxes for recycling were full to overflowing, and the house pet, Hugo, a large black Afghan-Labrador mix, seemed intent on making his somewhat lonely male presence felt.

The tofu was better than Meg expected. Once she got over trying to pretend it tasted like meat, she actually began to enjoy it. Perhaps she wouldn't have to go on a junk-food binge after all. And there was mochi, the hot puffed rice, so rich and moist it was almost like a "real" dessert with a little butter on it.

It was such a high for Meg to be in the company of other women even when she wasn't always able to keep up with the conversation. So she just sat among them, quiet, happy, as she stored fragments of conversation. Wanda and Linda had been together for a couple of years and had met at another Cris Williamson concert; it was an anniversary of sorts for them. Trish and Pat were single, information to file away for possible future use. Mostly the talk was about the concert and other women's festivals each had attended.

It was well into the night before Meg learned what her dinner companions did in the outside world. Trish was a carpenter, Wanda a C.P.A., Pat a counselor at the women's health center, which included coordinating clinic escorts. She never did find out how Linda made her living. Meg found it interesting that in the straight world she had come from so recently "What do you do?" was one of the first questions asked following introductions. It served both as a conversational gambit and as a ranking system. Among lesbians, it seemed almost an afterthought, a woman carpenter getting just as much admiration as a woman lawyer.

Finally, one woman after another began yawning. Meg's watch showed 1:58 a.m. No wonder they were all fading.

"Well, I need to get to bed. I have to work tomorrow—I mean today," Wanda said.

Pat added, "Me, too. The volunteer scheduled for the afternoon called in sick, so I have to cover for her, plus finish my regular work before lunch."

After a quick clean-up, piling the dishes in the sink for someone—hopefully—to wash later, the five wandered off to their bedrooms. Wanda, Linda and Trish went upstairs. Pat and Meg went through the living room and into the shop through the inside entrance. As they passed through the hallway, Meg glanced out the front window. The drunk was still there. She hoped he would be gone by morning.

Meg rolled out her sleeping bag, then tried to open the bathroom door but something was blocking it. Toothbrush in hand, she tiptoed back through the house in the dark, hoping she wouldn't stumble over Hugo. Fumbling, Meg found the light switch and pulled. Nothing. "Damn," she said out loud. "This was broken the last time I was here." She stood in the dark for a few moments, until her eyes adjusted. It was good that she had. Gradually, she made out the forms of two bicycles jammed up against the door into the shop, carpentry tools lying on the floor, and a broken wooden chair. After she shuffled to the sink, Meg brushed her teeth, hoping she wouldn't have to use the bathroom again until daylight. She was happy to get back to her bed uninjured.

She lay down as quietly as she could, not knowing if Pat was asleep. A shaft of outside light shone directly across her face, blinding her. Raising herself on her elbow, Meg looked around the room for a switch.

"Too bad about that," a soft voice came from the nearby bed. "You'll just have to make do or move your pillow."

"I didn't wake you, did I?"

Pat yawned. "Uh-uh. I was just thinking about having to take tomorrow's shift at the clinic. Mondays aren't a lot of fun. The anti's get all worked up in church on Sundays and come out with a vengeance Mondays to show their disapproval of our existence."

"What are anti's?"

"Well, they like to call themselves pro-life and us pro-abortion. We prefer to call ourselves pro-choice and them anti-choice."

"Are you in the clinic in the northwest?" Meg turned on her side to try to get away from the light.

"That's the one. Do you know it?"

"Not exactly. I drove by there earlier this evening. I was lost. The slogans on the walls really jarred me."

Pat's anger was thinly veiled. "Pretty vicious, aren't they?"

"Yes, they are. It must be pretty intimidating to be there when the protesters are out in force."

"Yes," Pat answered with vehemence in her voice. "But I'll be damned if I let those self-righteous bigots tell me what to do with my body—or any other woman's."

Meg chuckled. "Most of them would probably be more than happy to tell you that you already *are* damned."

"Well, if there is a heaven, they're going to be in for a big surprise when they find out that God didn't appoint them judges of other people's morality."

"Do you have any kids?" Meg asked, wanting to learn why this woman had such conviction in her voice.

Sensing where Meg's question was coming from, Pat said softly, "No, but my younger sister died in 1972 after an illegal abortion, and I sure as hell won't stand by and let it happen to anyone else."

"I'm sorry, Pat. I wish there was something I could do."

"Do you mean it, or are you just talking?"

That was pretty direct. Meg replied in kind. "I think I mean it. It took me a long time to get to the pro-choice position because it's never affected me personally, and the Catholic

Church has an adamantly pro-life, I, er, mean anti-choice, stance. It wasn't till I left the church that I could look at it with different eyes. What do the clinic escorts do?"

"We ask a minimum commitment of four hours per month. There's a three-hour training program that teaches volunteers how to handle the protesters and protect the clients. Are you interested?"

Meg's voice was thoughtful. "I think so, but I'm not sure I'm ready."

"How long are you going to be in town?"

"Why?"

"If you want to find out if you're ready, why don't you come with me tomorrow?"

"Would I have to do anything?"

"No. You could watch me and see how I handle it. You wouldn't have to be directly involved."

"Sure, why not? I don't have to go home till tomorrow evening."

"Great! Well, we better get some sleep. It sounds like we both have a busy day tomorrow."

"Sounds like it," Meg answered, a smile on her face, but a knot beginning to form in her stomach at the thought of facing the protesters. "Sleep well, Pat."

"You too, Meg." In a few minutes, Pat was asleep. Meg lay quietly, listening to her soft, regular breathing. Somewhere Jody lay in bed. Probably lonely. Probably restless. That afternoon on the beach, that afternoon out of time . . . had it been a dream? Did Jody ever think of it . . . of her? Meg pushed her sleeping bag aside and sat up. What could she do with this yearning she had, this yearning to be there for Jody, to comfort her?

The shop was full of pillows; she found a big, fluffy one. Snuggling back in her bag, she held the pillow close, cradling it like a lover. Under her breath, she sang, "'I'll hold you while angels sing you to sleep . . .'"

9
Lull Before the Storm

All too soon, the morning sun replaced the harsh outside light, finally convincing Meg that she could no longer hide from the day. As soon as she remembered where she was, she glanced across the room to see if Pat were still there. The bed was empty. Glancing at her watch, Meg saw that it was almost ten, and she had to be out of the shop in a few minutes or she would be part of the floor show. She smiled to herself, thinking of an advertisement that could be placed in front of her reclining body: "Lesbian sleeps well on futon, despite traffic noise and harsh lights."

She was still in her concert sweater, having discarded her jeans as soon as her sleeping bag had gotten warm enough. There they were, lying somewhat neatly on the floor next to the futon. Quickly, she pulled them on, rolled up her pillow in her sleeping bag and headed back into the main part of the house, all the while wondering where Pat had gotten to. Passing Pat's bed, she spotted a note on the pillow:

"Meg,

"You seemed so deeply asleep, I didn't have the heart to wake you. I had to get to work. If you're still interested in going with me to the clinic, meet me for lunch at Old Wives' Tales at noon.

"—Pat"

There was still time to think about it—but first, breakfast. Meg wandered into the kitchen to forage, the house empty except for her. Fortunately, someone had done a quick tidy-up of last night's dinner dishes, but she had no idea where things were kept. A quick glance through the shelves told her what she had already suspected—no coffee anywhere in sight. Herb tea was all right for dinner but not for breakfast, so she decided to go to the quick-stop market next door, happy to see that the drunk on the doorstep had disappeared with the dawn.

Returning with a steaming cup of coffee and two Hostess cupcakes, Meg sat out on the front porch, enjoying watching the people passing by. There were a few business types, looking important and walking fast, but mostly it was a mix of retired people, housewives with an occasional pre-school kid in tow, or a wino or con artist. Whenever she noticed the approach of the last two, she tried to look invisible, focusing her attention on some distant spot, hoping they would not notice or approach her. Her middle-class, suburban upbringing had not prepared her for the poverty and aggressiveness of some of the inhabitants of the city.

After nearly an hour of people-gazing, Meg felt relaxed and ready for the day, so she turned her mind again to the family planning clinic. Soon she was deep in conversation with herself, her adventurous side taking the lead. "I don't see why you can't just go down there and see it for yourself. What's the big deal?"

Her cautious side marshalled convincing arguments on the other side. "What do you mean? Every time I listen to you I find myself in strange and uncomfortable situations. Remember the women's prison where I preached?"

"Big deal. You survived, didn't you? Anyway, you keep talking about how important women's issues are. Don't you mean it?" the other voice challenged.

"Well, yes, I guess I do," her cautious side sighed, sensing defeat.

"Well, then, better get on with it. We have less than an hour to get to the restaurant."

"Oh, all right!" Meg said out loud as she got up from the stoop, her outburst startling a passerby. Smiling sheepishly, she went back into the house to freshen up before going to the restaurant.

A few minutes later, Meg was out the door, still wearing her slightly rumpled levis. She had discarded her sweater for a large red T-shirt which said, "Goddesses are not anorexic," with a red flannel shirt over it. If it got too hot, she could always discard the long-sleeved shirt, but she needed to keep the protection of her warrior-goddess amulet today.

In no time at all, Meg was pulling into the parking lot of the restaurant, just off one of the bridges connecting the two parts of the city, divided by the Willamette River. The lunch crowd was already pouring in, so Meg claimed a small table overlooking the street. She sat facing the door so she could see Pat when she came in. She was deep into the menu when the large table next to her began to fill with women, coming in one or two at a time. As she tried to decide between a vegetarian garden burger and a more traditional enchilada, snippets of their conversation floated by.

"Damn it, the *Gazette* did it to us again! There were over two hundred people picketing the Metro Bus Lines, and it didn't even get a footnote!"

"Well, I sure hope the bus boycott will make them take us—or at least our spending power—seriously. Three members of Quack are going to the Metro policy meeting tonight."

What in hell is 'Quack'? Meg wondered. It sounded more like an environmentalist group than anything else. Puzzled, she glanced up at the door, spotting Pat entering at last, just a little after noon. She was a handsome woman, slight in build, a bit under 5'4", dark short hair with a natural wave and a little dyke tail. Spotting Meg, Pat moved with assurance and grace through the lunchtime crowd.

"Sorry I'm a bit late. Have you ordered yet?"

"No. I can't decide between the garden burger and enchilada. What do you suggest?"

"Oh, I usually get a bowl of their Hungarian mushroom soup, the salad bar, with coffee and rice pudding if I'm feeling particularly decadent."

"Sounds good. I think I'll join you."

On their way to the salad bar, they had to pass by the table with the increasingly large and vocal group of women, now numbering around ten. One of the latecomers was adding her thought.

"I'm tired of being treated like a moral leper. People thinking they have to hide their children from me. I can't believe people found offense in that AIDS poster."

"I agree with you, Amanda, but you need to remember . . ."

Unfortunately, Pat and Meg were now out of earshot. Taking the opportunity, Meg whispered, "Pat, what is all of this I hear about the boycott and poster? And what is 'Quack'?"

Pat smiled. "I guess when you're in the middle of it, it's hard to remember that not everyone knows what's going on. Let's get our soup, and I'll fill you in when we get back to the table."

The soup looked rich, resplendent with mushrooms and paprika. Filling her bowl to the rim and balancing a plate of rolls and margarine, Meg managed to get back to the table without spilling anything.

"Okay, fill me in. Start with 'Quack.' Some women have T-shirts with ducks on them. What does it mean?"

"Actually, it's an acronym, QUAC, standing for Queers United Against Closets. It began because most of the lesbian and gay community thinks that the *Gazette* has been unfair to us, either by ignoring us completely or just mouthing right-wing platitudes about us and our morally bankrupt lifestyles. Its intransigent attitude has provided a focus for political activity, not just about Measure 8 and AIDS, but other city- and statewide issues."

"What about the bus boycott?" Meg continued, leaning forward.

"The AIDS Project has been developing ads that are directed at the gay male population. The major national campaigns have focused only on heterosexuals, and this project wanted to create ads for the group at highest risk. There was a poster, funded by state money, that showed a couple of young gay men looking into each other's eyes, one with his arm around the other, both smiling. The caption said, 'We can live. Together.' In small print was information about safe sex and cooperation among the general population."

"What was so bad about that?" Meg asked.

"It struck me as pretty harmless, but I think that when it gets right down to it, the straight population just doesn't want to admit that there can be beautiful and loving male relationships. They would rather hang on to their stereotypes of gay men as child molesters and sexually promiscuous."

"What happened then?"

"Metro Bus Lines started to get phone protests as soon as the posters went up on some of their buses. Once we heard about it, we began calling in too, but they decided to play it safe and pulled all the ads. We sent representatives to their office, the AIDS Project director called them, we went to public meetings, but we couldn't reverse the trend. Even the *Gazette* ran an editorial by Ted Reiner, an associate editor, that supported Metro's position."

"Wow, that's pretty heavy-duty. I guess spending the afternoon observing the protesters at the clinic is the least I can do. I guess I'm ready to go ahead with it."

Pat smiled. "Good for you, Meg. I need to be there in fifteen minutes, so we'd better get going."

10
The Hurricane's Eye

After paying the bill, Pat and Meg went out to the parking lot, the QUAC group still going strong. Pat spoke first. "Why don't we take my car? I can drop you off back here later."

"Sounds great." Meg was relieved, having no desire to deal with lunchtime traffic in downtown Portland.

Soon they were heading west in Pat's elderly VW bug, painted a garish orange. Meg took the chance to retreat into herself, thinking about the conflict she was about to enter, even if only on the sidelines for today. Cars pushed in on every side, each with its occupants sealed into their own private worlds, closed windows offering false and fragile protection from the outside world. Yet there was a hidden battle going on right in the city, and in towns and cities all across the nation, one that would break into any home, open any window no matter how tightly closed, shatter any false complacency. Women were on the front lines, their wombs the disputed territory, their lives and destinies riding on the outcome.

Meg sometimes longed for simpler days and easier chioces, but Thomas Wolfe was still right: no matter how painful it sounded, you can't go home again. There was simply no way to turn back to the days of "Father Knows Best" and "The Brady Bunch."

"We're almost there." Pat's voice jarred her back to the present. Coming out of her reverie, Meg noticed they were still several blocks from the clinic. Pat pulled over, deftly maneuvering her bug between two larger cars.

"Can't you get a bit closer to the clinic?" Meg wondered.

"I could, but some of the clinic staff's cars have been vandalized. I prefer keeping mine out of the line of fire. Speaking of the line of fire, are *you* ready for it?"

Meg managed a weak laugh. "No, but it's ready for me, so let's go before I change my mind."

It took only a couple of minutes at a fast walk before Meg could hear the picketers. At first, all she could hear was the angry stridence of their voices, then individual phrases separated out. "Baby-killers! Butchers!"

As they turned the corner, she could see them at last—a crowd of twenty or so, mostly women, two or three men in business suits looking stern and judgmental, three or four children, faces already having lost the look of innocence, leaning into their mothers for protection. They were bunched together, crowding the edge of the sidewalk, pushing against the invisible wall that defined the edge of their lawful space. They seemed to be primarily middle-class, with a couple on either side of the social spectrum, each face tight with hatred, jaws rigid, eyes glaring indiscriminate judgment. As she scanned their "righteous" visages, a tremor of dread coursed through Meg's body. Her fists clenched, her face became an immobile mask, her breathing almost stopped.

Pat, inured to this, seemed unaware of Meg's sudden shift in mood. "Why don't you wait down the block, Meg? If they see you with me, they'll harrass you, too. If it gets too hot and heavy for you, I'll meet you back at the car around five."

It was hard for Meg to get her jaws and mind moving again. "Ah . . . okay, Pat." Meg's voice trembled slightly. In an attempt to cover up her anxiety, she added, "Have a good day." Under the circumstances, that sounded like a particularly stupid remark, but it was the best she could do.

Smiling briefly at her, Pat set her shoulders and strode firmly past the protesters, refusing to make eye contact with them or be drawn into their taunts. As the crowd spotted her, they shifted their attention from the front door to her. "Bitch! Dyke! Man-hater!" Pat didn't even pause. God, Meg thought, she must have to do this every time. That took a lot of guts. She wondered if it got easier as time went on.

Well, as long as she was here, she might as well get comfortable. Four hours was a long time to stand on the corner. Looking around, Meg saw a salmon-colored rose bush in full bloom with a decorative log next to it. Cautiously, she approached the log, dividing her attention between the protesters and the house the plant was next to. All was quiet inside; no one seemed to be at home. So she sat down, trying to disappear into the bush, preparing herself for a long vigil.

She looked at her watch. One o'clock exactly. As she looked up again towards the clinic, she saw a disembodied hand remove the "Closed for Lunch" sign from the window. As it did, the chants from the crowd increased in their intensity.

Just at that moment, a light blue sedan drive by Meg's hideout, a tense but determined teenage male driving, a young woman in the passenger's seat. She looked neatly dressed, but she had obviously been crying and was clutching her purse to her chest as if to draw solace from it. As they neared the clinic, the young woman scrunched down in the seat, her head leaning toward the door, only her face showing. As it approached the clinic, the car slowed down, its blinker signalling. Spotting the car, the protesters turned as one, waving their signs over it as it passed, like an evil malediction, a rite of cursing.

The young man pulled into a vacant space, got out, went around to the passenger's side and opened the door. The woman, little more than a girl, perhaps 17 at most, looked terrified as the voices began to rise in intensity. "Don't go in. Don't kill your baby," a middle-aged woman pleaded. A well-dressed man shouted at her escort, "You could be a father today. Be a man, and don't kill your baby." Turning to fix a glance of pure hatred at them, the young man reached down to grasp his girlfriend's elbow, helping her from the car. As they approached the clinic, he placed his body between her and the crowd, putting his left arm around her shoulders and holding her close to him. The shouts increased as it became evident that they were going into the clinic.

"Baby-killers! Murderers!"

"Slut! Fornicator!"

Pat and another woman came out and wordlessly placed themselves on either side of the couple, forming a human cushion of protection.

Meg was frustrated. It was as if she had picked up an interesting novel and read sections of it, only to misplace it before she could finish. She wanted to know more—why the girl had gotten pregnant, how they had made the decision to have an abortion, if it was her first one (or last, for that matter), what impact it was going to have on the girl's life. But the closing door cut off all contact. This was real life, not a novel, and she could only guess. Whatever chain of events had led this couple to this door and through it, was not part of her life nor any of her business. As the door closed, Meg found her heart going out to them, and she sent them on their way with her blessing.

11
R and R at the Coast

Hours passed unnoticed by Meg, mesmerized by the human spectacle unfolding before her. Not wanting to call attention to herself, she moved only to stretch her legs and aching back, or to stay in the paltry shade of the rose bush as the temperature soared into the eighties.

Over and over the same scene was enacted. The crowd of protesters, periodically somnolent, became stimulated anew each time their prey pulled into the parking lot or the clinic door opened. Meg thought of sharks going into a feeding frenzy at the smell of blood. Given the choice, she wasn't sure that real sharks wouldn't be preferable. Except for the passage of the relentless sun across the bright afternoon sky, time seemed frozen in an endless and unresolved morality play.

"Meg!" A sharp voice brought her out of her near-hypnotic state. Startled, she turned around.

"Pat . . . I didn't see you leave the clinic."

"I came out the back door and walked around the block. I've had my fill of zealots for the day." Meg got up slowly and, trying to shake a feeling of sleepwalking, attempted to match Pat's brisk pace. "How did you enjoy it?" Pat looked at her curiously.

Meg was silent for a moment. "I'm not sure 'enjoy' is the right word. It was fascinating and powerful but very, very painful. My heart went out to those women I saw go into the clinic. It must be a hard decision to make. I'm glad I never had to."

Pat nodded. "I know what you mean. Are you still willing to take volunteer training?"

Meg sighed. "I guess it's time. I can't sit on the sidelines any longer."

"Great! I'll give you the number of the volunteer coordinator. Call him and take the training, then you can be scheduled."

The seats in Pat's car were unbearably hot. They got in with little yelps of pain, rolled down the windows, and drove across town in companionable silence. Meg was glad to see her truck sitting in front of the restaurant, waiting for her. After thanking Pat, she climbed gratefully into the cab. Soon she was on the freeway heading west, her mind disengaged, her hands driving automatically. The last two days had been more adventure than she had bargained for, and she was tired. She stopped for a few hours to see her kids—tired or not, she couldn't resist when she was this close—and then started the final leg of her homeward journey.

She was almost at the coast before she noticed the gas gauge hovering on the wrong side of empty and pulled into a little gas station. She checked her wallet and was discouraged to discover that she had only a dollar left. She opened the ash tray, where she kept her spare change, and dug out another seventy-five cents. She felt silly ordering a dollar and seventy-five cents' worth of gas and then counting out the change into the attendant's hand—the dollar bill, then one quarter, two dimes, four nickels and ten pennies. Her paycheck would be waiting when she got back to town; it wouldn't be a bad idea to swing by the motel and pick it up before she went home. Her spare tire was waiting, too; better retrieve it before the ten dollars went to something else.

The motel looked its usual shabby self, flakes of old green paint glinting in the last afternoon sun. Meg rang the bell on the counter in the office, and Mrs. Green bustled in from the adjoining living room, hoping for a customer. There were only two other cars in the lot. "Oh, it's you," Mrs. Green didn't try to hide her disappointment. "I guess you're here for your paycheck. I have it back here somewhere." As she rummaged under the counter, Meg made small talk.

"It seems like a slow day."

"It is, but I'm just as glad in a way. Mr. Green has bronchitis and has to stay in bed for awhile."

"I'm sorry to hear that," said Meg. "Say hello for me."

"Oh, here it is, dear." With one hand, Mrs. Green pushed back a stray strand of hair. "I'm feeling a little overwhelmed today. Mr. Green was supposed to start repainting the outside of the motel tomorrow, and I don't know when he can start now. I'm afraid the place is beginning to turn customers away."

"That's too bad. Maybe he'll be better by next week. I'll be in on Saturday. Well," Meg began backing towards the door, "I need to run a couple of errands. See you soon."

She could barely wait until she got to the truck to tear open her paycheck, accidentally ripping off the corner in her haste. She couldn't believe it! She had worked 48 hours in the last three weeks, and her take-home pay was only $143.72. It was going to be a thin month.

With assurance born of desperation, Meg, head held high, strode back into the office. Mrs. Green was still there, distractedly tidying up the counter area.

"Hello again," Meg said. "Look, I have a proposition for you. It sounds like Mr. Green isn't going to be back on his feet for awhile, and the motel needs painting now. I've done a lot"—(well, a little, but she could fake the rest)—" of house painting. I'd be willing to start the job until Mr. Green can take over, and I'd only charge," Meg took a deep breath, "six dollars an hour. That's less than a third what a professional painter would cost."

Mrs. Green perked up. "That's a good idea, dear. But I could only afford to pay you five." She sounded flustered. "Mind you, I know it's worth more than that, but business has really been slow the last couple of weeks."

Meg calculated quickly. That was better than what she was getting as a maid, and she needed the money. "It's a deal. I can start Wednesday." She needed a day off to recover from her trip to Portland.

"All right, dear. I'll expect you Wednesday morning at eight o'clock."

Feeling better about finances, Meg drove to the bank to deposit the check in the night deposit slot. She would put in $125 to cover overdue bills, saving $10 for the tire. That left $8.72 to spend on food. It was a good thing she had lots of dry beans, flour and rice at home. She would pick up some ground chuck and fresh vegetables and milk and make them stretch until another payday.

Next came the gas station. It was already almost seven, and there was only one attendant on duty. Gas stations made her nervous. She was glad Oregon was the only state that didn't allow self-service, so she didn't have to decide whether or not to pump her own gas. In the past, when she was married, she could accept help with simple things like checking the tire pressure and water and oil levels and cleaning windshields. Now it was as if she were earning her way into the community of women by insisting on doing these chores herself.

On reflection, Meg thought she had acquitted herself well in the matter of her flat tire. She had changed it herself, looked for obvious punctures, and brought it to the station with an aura of self-confidence that only another lesbian could see as still part facade. Taking a deep breath in preparation for her next bit part as super-dyke, Meg jumped down from the cab and made her way to the office.

"Hi, I was told my tire would be ready by now. My name is Meg Blake."

The young man, still in the throes of proving his manhood, glanced at her "tail" with a questioning look on his face, then looked at her left hand. Meg supposed it was to see if a ring made it clear she was someone's property. She secretly reveled in his obvious confusion.

"Oh, yeah, we have it back here." He wiped his grease-covered hands on his pants and found it on a rack in the shadows, then rolled the tire toward her through the middle of the grease-covered garage floor. "That'll be ten dollars, two more if you want me to mount it."

"No, thanks," Meg proclaimed proudly, handing him a ten. "I'll do it myself later tonight." She hoped he realized it was more a question of pride than the extra money. The attendant began to roll it to her truck, but Meg intervened. "That won't be necessary. I can get it." He looked deflated as she took the tire from him. Picking it up with one hand through the middle, Meg started toward the truck before she remembered there was something she wanted to ask and turned back again. "By the way, what caused the flat? I couldn't find any obvious punctures or anything like that."

The boy-man looked arrogant again. "You're lucky the tire didn't just fall apart, it's in such bad shape. It was hardly worth repairing. But it wasn't a nail hole. It was a slit right next to the hubcap."

That was odd. "Could a piece of glass or metal cause something like that? She figured she would have remembered if she had run over something that substantial.

"Not really. It looks like someone did it on purpose." He paused for effect, a superior smile on his face. "Maybe your old man did it."

Meg shot back caustically, "I'm not married." She threw the tire into the back of the truck, knowing full well he was thinking no one in his right mind would ever marry her. It wasn't until she was in the grocery store that Meg saw the humor of the situation: the young man trying to prove his manhood, she trying to prove her competence as a dyke. Maybe in some other lifetime they would laugh together about it, but probably not in this one.

It had been a long day, and she needed a good dinner. She hadn't eaten since noon, and it was already close to eight o'clock. As soon as she got home, she took a couple of tortillas out of the freezer and put them in the oven to warm. Then she sauteed some ground beef with an onion and part of a green pepper, grated some cheese, and within a few minutes had her meal prepared. Chopped up lettuce and tomato thrown over the tortillas and beef added her version of a gourmet touch. She took her plate out to the back porch, where she sat down on the stoop and leaned against the house, still warm against her back, to watch the sunset. The clouds were turning orange and gold, the rays of the sun dancing one last time on the water.

Later, full and relaxed, Meg got up reluctantly to deal with the tire. After she put her dishes in the kitchen sink, she rummaged in the closet for her grungiest pair of work jeans, then went out under the darkening sky. The night was still warm, a gentle breeze blowing off the ocean. She would miss the late summer nights but was also looking forward to her first winter storms.

After moving the truck as close to the porch light as possible, Meg mumbled to herself as she began her task. "Let's see now—tire iron, jack, flashlight . . . That ought to do it. Oh, I better put the truck in gear and put some rocks under the other tires." That accomplished, Meg proclaimed, for no one's ears but her own, "There, it actually looks like I know what I'm doing."

As she began the oddly pleasing task, she considered the slash. Who could have done something like that? She didn't have any enemies that she knew of, and she was quite sure that her "old man" wouldn't even think of it, much less do it. Theirs was still a close relationship, something that none of her few new acquaintances could either understand or accept. It just wasn't "politically correct" to be close to your former husband. They weren't even legally separated yet. If that offended people, it was just too bad. She was determined to move at her own pace.

The slash was probably just an act of vandalism, possibly perpetrated by teenage boys proving their bravery. Well, it could have been worse. There wasn't any use in continuing to worry about it.

In just a few minutes, Meg was lowering the jack, the repaired tire remounted. "Well, that's it. As good as new." Back in the cabin, she was suddenly hungry, her dinner only a dim memory. Opening the freezer, she rummaged around in its far corners, finally unearthing a small container of chocolate chip cookie dough. After she made some coffee, she stuck a big wooden spoon into the dough. What a marvelous taste! She could never understand why people insisted on baking the dough. This was surely ample reward for going to the clinic, picking up her first paycheck and changing a tire. Sitting on the side of her bed, she gave the spoon one last lick and then crawled in, falling asleep almost instantly with the taste of brown sugar and chocolate still in her mouth.

12
The Witch Doctor

Somehow she found time the next week, between painting the motel and cleaning its rooms, to spend an evening in Portland taking the nonviolence training required of clinic escorts. Staying busy kept her from thinking or feeling . . . or worrying about Jody. Would it ever feel right to call?

On the way home from Portland, Meg stopped to see the kids. Stacey was fascinated by the blue paint that now flecked her glasses; Meg let her hold them and scratch it off with her fingernails as she curled up beside her. Tom, a quiet, thoughtful young man, was intrigued by her stories of the clinic and the training.

"How about coming along for the ride, Tom? My first stint is next week." She and Tom used to stay up late at night talking about all sorts of things. Since Meg had moved out, Tom had become more and more withdrawn. Perhaps spending a day with him away from his sisters would allow them to connect more deeply than short visits to the home did.

"Well . . ."

She knew his shyness well. "It'll be fine. I've already driven by the clinic. There's a store across the street. We can park there, and you can watch me from the car."

"Okay," he agreed. "And, mom, can I drive?"

"You've got a deal. See you next week."

Meg knew Tom was caught in the crossfire of her changing beliefs; all she could do was provide him with a chance to draw his own conclusions about reproductive choice.

The next Saturday, Meg was pleased to see Tom waiting outside for her. She was startled anew at this boy-man somehow still her son, at his nearly six-foot frame, at the hint of light blond stubble on his face. It was odder still to sit in the passenger's seat and look across at him driving so skillfully, considering he had just gotten his learner's permit.

Finally, Meg found the opening she had been waiting for. "Are you confused about why I'm becoming an escort for a family planning clinic?"

He paused before answering. "Yes, I am. It's quite a switch for you, mom."

"Yes, it is. After a few months working at the women's shelter . . ." She paused. "Look . . . I don't want to influence you . . . I want you to come to your own conclusions." He nodded imperceptibly. After all, his parents had been saying the same sort of thing since he was in kindergarten.

They rode in silence until Meg directed Tom to the right off-ramp. As they drew near the clinic, Meg spoke. "Pull over here, Tom. You can park next to that tree at the edge of the parking lot. That should give you a front-row seat."

Speaking softly, Meg got ready to get out of the truck. She certainly didn't want to draw attention to it, or to Tom, for that matter. "Tom, there's change in the ashtray if you want to go into the store to get a drink. Make sure to lock up the truck if you have to leave it. See you in a couple of hours."

So far, there were just two or three picketers; when none of the protesters was looking her way, Meg quietly opened the door, stepped out, shut it and walked away quickly. She got by the first protester without too much trouble, but the second, a woman dressed in stone-washed jeans, brown cowboy boots, expensive padded coat and scarf, was more alert. She turned on Meg and said in a strident, sarcastic voice, "The dykes are out in force today!" Meg almost started laughing, since, for her, being called a dyke was a compliment. It always made her feel incredibly proud. But something in the woman's hate-distorted face showed it to be a supreme insult.

A few more strides placed Meg in the safety of the injunction zone. Thanks to the ruling of a Portland judge, there was a "safe" zone extending 12-1/2 feet in each direction from the clinic door all the way to the sidewalk that was off-limits to the protesters. One of the clinic escorts smiled while opening the door to the clinic.

Meg smiled in return. "No, I want the other door. I'm an escort."

Once inside, she breathed a sigh of relief. The dingy office offered a welcome sanctuary. Too bad she just couldn't sit there and somehow be useful. Oh well, it couldn't be as bad as all that, could it? Picking up an orange vest which said "Clinic Escort," Meg buttoned it over her T-shirt, took a deep breath and opened the door to the outside.

When she found the woman in charge, identifiable by her walkie-talkie and clipboard, Meg approached her. "Hi, I'm Meg. This is my first time as an escort."

"Welcome," the woman smiled encouragingly. "My name is Linda. It's pretty quiet so far, but I expect it to heat up later. Why don't you start out here, in front of the door, and get your feet wet? Later on, I may need you to be on the corner in the middle of the protesters. Usually, Patricia and Ivan show up later, and things can get pretty hot out there on the corner."

That was fine with Meg. She supposed two thin lines of chalk, 12-1/2 feet on either side, weren't much protection, but it was more than the escorts on the corner had, and they were already surrounded by newly arrived picketers shouting in their faces. Standing as close to the door as she could while still being able to look for potential clients, Meg surreptitiously examined the three protesters nearest her. One was dressed completely in a yellow slicker, mumbling under his breath and talking only with other picketers. He had a camera but mostly seemed interested in taking pictures of the bus zone posters in front of the clinic; Meg couldn't fathom why. Another seemed a little less bizarre. Middle-aged, bordering on good-looking, he stopped bystanders from time to time, engaging them in an earnest but quiet debate. A third, also middle-aged, but with short brown hair and a badly pock-marked face, looked as if he would be more of a problem. He held a picture of a fetus with the American flag in the background; his pockets were full of pamphlets and full-color pictures of aborted fetuses. He stood as close as he could get to the line and kept trying to draw Meg into a confrontation.

"Hey, lady, how many abortions have you had? Don't you ever want a baby to dandle on your knee?" Dandle? Come on! It was all she could do to keep from replying, "I've never had an abortion, and my baby is sitting across the street watching your antics." Instead, she just focused on a point in the distance, carefully guarding her facial muscles.

Soon a couple of little boys, around 8 or 9, pushing bicycles, started coming down the sidewalk towards her. Right before they reached the chalked-in area, the man with the sign stopped them. "Ask those people there in the orange vests if they have birthdays. Do you have birthdays? They want to make sure the babies of the mothers going into this clinic don't have birthdays. They kill babies in there. This is an evil place." Not knowing how to respond, the boys kept silent as they wheeled their bicycles away. It was really hard for Meg to keep from entering the fray, but she bit her tongue, knowing it was useless to try to argue with the man.

But how she wanted to talk with the kids! Yet, what could she tell them? Yes, there were abortions being performed in there, and no, not all kids, even those already born, were wanted. She hoped those two boys didn't know that yet, but they would someday. Kids by the tens of thousands were sleeping with their families in old cars, going without medical care or proper nutrition. All the Reagan administration had said about it was that people slept on streets because they wanted to. Other children were beaten, sexually assaulted, sometimes even killed, every hour of the day, and society as a whole wasn't particularly concerned.

The first hour went by quickly, only one protester violating the injunction zone. He kept walking over the chalk line, much like a little kid testing authority, then was told he was breaking the law. Whenever Linda tried to take his picture, he would put his sign in front of his face and step back over the line. From time to time, Meg glanced down the corner to make sure Tom was all right. Then she saw an old bronze car, covered with *Yes on Measure 8* stickers, the anti-gay initiative, pull up beside him. She was too far away to intervene unless it was absolutely necessary, but she kept watch.

A man got out, walked around her truck, looked at the bumper stickers, then went around to the passenger's window and leaned over Tom. Meg tensed, ready to intervene if necessary. After all, even if Tom was a half-foot taller than she was, he was still her son, and she would protect him.

After a minute or so, the man turned away, grabbed a sign through his front seat and marched across the street towards Meg.

Meg finally got Tom's attention, flashing him a peace sign. He flashed one back to her, so she guessed he would be okay until her shift was over. Then someone tapped her lightly on the shoulder. It was the escort coordinator.

"Well, Meg, are you ready to go onto the front lines? Their big guns are just arriving, and I would like to relieve the escorts on the corner."

Meg swallowed nervously. "Sure, I guess I'm as ready as I'll ever be."

Walking to the corner, she approached the other escorts. "I'll handle this for awhile. Why don't some of you go on inside and get something to drink?" Two left, leaving her with a middle-aged, pleasant-looking man, who introduced himself as Reggie. As soon as the two escorts left, a large car pulled up to the curb. A man in a white lab coat with a paper bag over his head emerged from the driver's side.

Spotting Meg and Reggie through his eye slits, he strode up to them. Then, shaking his hands in the air, he began chanting, "Ooga booga, ooga booga, ooga booga," as he leaped into the air and pranced around, much to the admiration of his cohorts. It took all that Meg and Reggie had not to burst out laughing.

Finally tired of their lack of response, the man wandered away. "What was all that about?" Meg asked Reggie.

"Oh, they think that pagans are in back of the abortion movement, and he was mimicking a witch doctor."

Meg was shocked. "Do they honestly believe that pagan rituals are like that? It looks more like a grade-B movie made in the fifties."

"Not only that, but they also think pagans steal babies to sacrifice at their circles."

Meg, remembering the beautiful and healing circles she had been to, couldn't even reply. She slipped her hand under her shirt for a moment to grasp the silver stylized goddess, warm from nestling between her breasts, that hung from her neck. How could everything get so turned around?

13
The Woman in the Blue Quilt Coat

After the "witch doctor" left, probably to return later in street clothes, there was a lull in the action, each side gathering strength for the next encounter. Needing a break, Meg turned to Reggie. "I'm going to get a cup of coffee. Want one?"

Reggie smiled. "Sure, black. Thanks."

"Can you manage by yourself, or should I send reinforcements?"

"I'll be okay. Just don't take too long."

Meg turned abruptly and walked quickly back to the door of the lounge, the picketers thrown off guard by her speed. Once inside the door, she took a breath and dropped into a chair. She was numb, in shock, puzzled by the hatred these total strangers held for her. Images of Martin Luther King and Gandhi floated in her mind, issuing their challenge to love. But right now, all she could do was stand up to these hostile people, eyeball to eyeball, do her job, and try not to hate them back.

After pouring a cup of coffee for Reggie and another for herself, Meg opened the door, bracing herself for another stint on the front lines. She marched back briskly to her post, a cup of coffee in each hand. As soon as she got there, the woman who had called her "dyke" turned suddenly, as if she could sense Meg's return. Taking two steps forward, she planted her expensive pumps on the pavement and shouted directly into Meg's face.

"You lesbians, we've got your number! Did you know lesbianism is going to be illegal soon in the state of Oregon? Measure 8 is going to pass and will show you people what we think of you. Lesbians hate kids and men. This is a Christian nation, and that means everybody either has to convert or leave this country."

Getting no response from Meg, she turned on Reggie. "You know, you're not even human. You're humanoid. So we can hate you. You're a bunch of brown shirts, and your days are numbered. Pretty soon we're going to put you all in prison or execute you. And your hero, Margaret Sanger. What do you know about her? You claim you're liberal and educated. Why don't you go to the public library and read about her? She was a Rosicrucian and a Theosophist and had sex with anything she could get her hands on."

Tired of the haranguing, Meg changed her tactics. Instead of staring off into the distance, she stared at the woman directly. At first, the woman stared back, but Meg was determined that this was one contest she would win. The escorts might not be allowed to speak back, but no one had said anything about staring. After a minute or two, the woman began faltering. Unflinching, Meg held her eyes steady until the woman could take no more and turned her attention to the passing traffic.

Then Meg caught a glimpse of blue out of the corner of her eye. Oh no, another protester! This one was marching towards the corner with a sign that said, "Honk if you hate abortion!" In her other hand, she held a shocking pink cassette tape recorder spewing forth fundamentalist gospel music. She clutched the hood of her quilted, light blue coat tightly around her face, a few strands of blond hair escaping. It seemed odd, since it was getting so hot. Maybe the coat was some sort of protection. Meg was close enough to see a large diamond on her ring finger.

The woman spotted a couple of teenage girls—one blonde, the other a redhead—headed towards the clinic and launched into an attack. "Don't go in there! Don't murder your babies. You're sluts, hear me? Sluts! Fornicators, God is going to send you to hell! Does your mother know you're here? What would she think if she knew you were killing her grandchild?"

The older girl, perhaps 18, turned on her in wrath. "You bitch! Mind your own business!"

Meg glanced at the clinic windows. "Reggie, the noise is getting out of hand. I'm going to see if I can get them into the escort lounge."

She walked up behind the girls, who were still yelling insult for insult. The woman in the blue quilted coat turned to stare at her, and Meg found herself looking into a hauntingly familiar face. Where had she seen it? She put one hand on each of the girls' shoulders. "Why don't you come inside and have some coffee?" Her hand on the blonde's arm, she gently began moving her towards the door. Meg had to suppress a chuckle as she saw herself as a sheepdog separating the sheep.

Inside, the older one let off steam. "Who does that bitch think she is? I'm not even here for an abortion." She was tall, thin, with long bright red fingernails and streaked blond hair that fell past her shoulders. "What in hell does she know about my mom? She was always strict with us. She raised us all by herself. She's a waitress. She knows I'm on birth control. All she needs is another mouth to feed."

Meg turned to the younger one, who was now sitting on the couch. "What about you? I have a daughter about your age."

The young woman looked up; freckles covered her face, red curly hair framed it. "I'm not pregnant now. But last year . . ." She shook her head and looked away. "It was my first year in high school . . . My boyfriend took off, and my parents threatened to throw me out. I came here." She turned back to Meg, her chin up. "I'm going to make sure I don't get pregnant again until I'm ready." Meg was struck by her, so worldly wise, so innocent underneath it all.

"We're here for our friend." The older one glanced at the clock. "She's in there now . . . Her appointment was half an hour ago." The two went up to the receptionist together, leaving Meg a moment to sit down on the tattered sofa. Where had she seen that woman before? Maybe if she could just let her mind wander, it would take her where she needed to go. It was a recent memory, so Meg methodically began going through the last few months. Just when she was about to give up, feeling guilty about her prolonged absence from the front lines, it came to her. Walking on a beach . . . summer, early one Saturday afternoon . . . She was at a gathering of women. Why, of course! It was the woman sitting off by herself, the one with the pristine white blouse, black polyester pants, and glimmering ring—the one who had seemed so out of place.

Meg went outside, glad to find the coordinator right beside the door, talking on her walkie-talkie with the clinic upstairs. When she finished, Meg spoke. "I was wondering what you know about that woman over there in the blue coat. Is she a regular?"

"You bet. I can't remember a Saturday she's missed, but I'm not here all the time. She's usually here Thursday evenings, too. Her name is Patricia Johnston, and she's as much a zealot as they come. She just lost a lawsuit against the clinic. She owes thousands to an employee she accused of having AIDS. Why do you need to know?"

"It's not important . . . it's just odd. I saw her on the beach this summer on a Saturday afternoon. It doesn't really matter."

"Hey, wait a minute! It'll only take a minute to check our records. We have to keep them on the protesters we know, and Patricia certainly qualifies."

"No, really, it's not important. It's time for me to get out to the corner again."

Linda glanced at her watch. "It's almost one. We shouldn't be getting any more clients today. Why don't you just go on home? I'll make sure the few women left upstairs get escorted safely back to their cars. It looks like you survived your first day here. Do you plan on coming back?"

"It's been quite a day. I still can't believe how these people twist things." Meg took a slow, deliberate breath. "But you can be sure I'm coming back. They aren't going to get any free shots at this place without my doing something about it."

"Good for you! Make sure you sign up for another shift before you go. And thanks for coming."

Outside, her truck looked empty until she was right beside it. Tom had slouched down as far as his long legs would let him. Meg took the wheel, and neither of them spoke till the clinic was well behind them. "Ma . . . I gotta stop for something." He glanced, deadpan, at her. "A lifetime supply of condoms."

"Glad to see you planning ahead."

They both grinned. Some of the tension from the morning dissolved. Meg continued. "Oh, by the way, what was that protester saying to you earlier today?"

"Oh, he asked me if I knew I was sitting in an anti-theistic truck." Tom smiled. "I guess he was referring to your 'Trust in

God/She will provide' bumper sticker. I guess only males can still be God. Then he kept on, wanting to know if I thought God was a woman. I just told him I was sitting there reading."

Then Tom leaned forward, his face growing tense. "Then, mom, he asked me if my old lady was inside getting an abortion. At first, I thought he meant you,"—Tom had not yet begun to date—"but later I realized he thought I had gotten my girlfriend pregnant. When I finally figured it out, I got really angry."

"Well, Tom, I was a bit worried for you at first, but it looked like you were handling it okay. What's your take on the situation now?"

He looked out the window. "They're vicious. They're . . . I dunno . . . crazy." He looked back at her for a moment, his face earnest. "Why? Why are they like that?"

She shook her head, feeling the same anguish she had experienced when the little boys had wheeled their bikes by. "I guess maybe they're scared." She sighed. "But, really, I don't know . . . I really don't know."

14
Malice Aforethought

Meg could hardly wait to get home, but Stacey was waiting on the front porch, as usual, her sad face letting Meg know that her short visit couldn't erase the pain and abandonment she saw there. "Mom," Stacey pleaded with her whole body, "come into my room so we can have some 'girl talk.' I just got a new tape, and there's this really cute guy in my class, and I think he likes me."

Three hours later, Meg pulled up thankfully in front of her cabin, slipped the mail from its box and let herself in, hungry for the comfort of her familiar nest. She dumped the mail on the couch, forgotten, as she picked out some fir and alder logs and got a fire blazing. This night in particular she needed its warm presence. Rummaging through her tapes, she found her favorite bathing music, "Pachelbel's Canon," and put it on at full volume. Then Meg poured herself a tall glass of Dr. Pepper and walked slowly into the bathroom.

She was so tired, drained of vitality. She felt physically violated by the protesters' hate. It seemed to cling to her skin and penetrate her body. Shuddering in remembrance, Meg turned the water on as hot as she could stand it, hoping that heat and a healthy dose of soap would wash away the venom she had been bathed in all day. After dropping her clothes in a heap, Meg climbed into the tub and slowly sank back.

At first, unable to find her "off" switch, all she could do was keep playing back the events of the day. Soon, though, the water reached her shoulders, which ached from being held so tightly. The heat penetrated deeply, loosening and soothing, allowing the music to work its magic. How could anyone hold on to anger and pain when "Pachelbel's Canon" spilled its chords into even the far corners of the little cabin? The soft, clear violins lifted her spirits as the trumpets poured power back into her nearly defeated body. There she stayed, until the hot water was used up and the last, lingering chords of music had faded away.

Feeling clean and whole again, Meg reluctantly got out of the tub, pulling her threadbare bathrobe on as she made her way into the living room. After clearing a space for herself on the couch, she gathered up the mail. The bills and ads she placed in a pile on the floor. They could wait. There was one personal letter, its still childlike scrawl identifying her oldest child, Alyson. "Dear Mom, don't forget you said you'd be at the athletic awards dinner next week. Come early! See you next week. Your daughter, Alyson."

Meg laughed aloud, remembering a time not far in the past when Alyson, angered by what she had perceived as Meg's betrayal of the family, had signed just her name to her short and bitter notes. Meg still felt some guilt about leaving, but she and Mark had made the best decision possible for the kids when she told him she was a lesbian and had to find out what that meant. Before going on, Meg went over to the desk to make sure she had next week's date marked on the calendar.

That left the local paper. Was it remotely possible that something interesting might be happening? Pedestrian accidents involving unwary tourists, beach clean-up days and clam and salmon bakes seemed to be the staples of summer news. Well, right now a little boredom might not be so bad. After throwing another log on the fire and putting her feet up on the couch, Meg pulled the rubber band from around the paper and shot it into a corner of the room, shook the paper out and opened it to the front page.

The headline jumped out at her: "Investigation Shows Newbridge Bay Tragedy No Accident." What? Sally must have been right. It was bad enough that Susan had died, but murder? The article continued:

"'The state criminologist's office has just released the results of its investigation of the death of Susan Callahan, who died when the van she was riding in plunged into the ocean in Newbridge Bay last July 17, late Saturday evening.

"While her death was caused by drowning, as originally reported, it is no longer being considered accidental. Her blood alcohol level was .13, .05 over the legal limit. Although she was not driving, her intoxication may have been a contributing factor in her inability to exit the vehicle once it was submerged.

"The victim was found still held by her seatbelt, her left hand clutching the emergency brake, which was pulled all the way out. Further investigation revealed that the brake cable had been severed.

"The District Attorney's office has issued a statement that a full investigation is in progress. Viewing it as a possible homicide, the D.A., John Kingsley, has said that he will spare no effort to discover how Ms. Callahan met her death. The other woman involved in the accident is being questioned, but no charges have been filed."

Meg sat, stunned, the newspaper clutched in her lap. Perhaps the rumors that Jody and Susan had been having diufficulties were true, but Jody seemed too sane and well-balanced to resort to violence to solve her problems. Or could she be as wrong about Jody as she had been about Kim? That was too painful to think about, so Meg brushed it aside. Time to call Crystal again.

Without giving herself time to think, Meg dialed. Four, five times it rang, Meg drumming her fingers across the desk. Come on, come on, answer!, she silently willed the woman down the coast.

"Hello?" a groggy voice answered after the tenth ring.

"Oops . . . sounds like I woke you . . . again . . ." Meg apologized.

"What time is it anyway?" the querulous voice asked. "And who is this?"

Meg glanced at the kitchen clock, which she could barely make out. "Uh, sorry, it's almost eleven. And this is Meg Blake again. I seem to have gotten into the habit of waking you up whenever I call."

"Oh, hi, Meg." The voice warmed up considerably. "What's the matter? You sound upset."

Meg gained reassurance from Crystal's voice. "I just found out about the investigation—you know, Susan's death—and I'm worried about Jody and how she's taking it. I wondered if you knew anything."

"She's taking it hard . . . it's a mess, Meg. Can you imagine losing your lover and then being questioned by the police . . . and on top of it, all your private life is suddenly everybody's business? You can't go in a shop here without somebody starting to talk about the 'lesbian murder.'"

Meg felt her pulse quicken. "Damn it! I suppose people are going to blow this all out of proportion. It's so unfair!"

"If you care, why don't you call her?" Crystal challenged.

Meg sat, stunned. "Me . . . call her . . ." she fumbled. "There must be other people . . ."

Crystal sighed. "At first, she closed down and pushed us away, but she was just starting to come out of her shell when this new stuff hit. You wouldn't believe this, but . . . well, most of her friends were Susan's friends too. Really, they were more Susan's friends. Jody's always been more of a loner. And they're not sure . . . with this stuff about murder . . . and so now they've pulled away. Not everyone—not me—but, well, we all knew Susan, and even if we believe in Jody, now she doesn't want us around, like she thinks maybe we secretly suspect her. But you didn't know Susan, so, I dunno . . . It's a mess, Meg. It's really a mess."

Meg's mind was reeling. "So, you think maybe I could help because I didn't know Susan?"

"It's worth a try, Meg. I mean, if you really want to. It's a lot to ask of somebody, to get mixed up in this mess."

"Oh, I want to!" Meg was rooting frantically among the papers on her desk, looking for a pen. She found a felt-tip and wrote the number Crystal gave her in large print right across the face of her blotter, not wanting to take the chance of misplacing it. "Thanks, Crystal, for everything. Well," she took a deep breath, then said resolutely, "I guess I better be going. I've got a phone call to make."

Not even pausing for breath, Meg dialed Jody's number. The first ring was cut short as the phone was picked up. "Who is this?" The voice was terse and guarded.

"Um, hi, this is Meg Blake. I met you at the beach, at the gathering, uh, last month . . ." She was greeted by silence, and her meager confidence faded. "Look, I really didn't want to disturb you. Maybe I could call you later."

"Meg." Jody paused for a moment, as though just now taking in who it was. "Hi. I guess I sound pretty weird . . . I've been getting a lot of vicious phone calls since the paper came out. I probably shouldn't even pick up the phone, but that makes me feel so isolated."

"Oh, God, I'm sorry. People can be real jerks sometimes. Did I wake you?"

Jody's voice still had an edge. "Don't worry about it . . . I'm not exactly sleeping like a baby these days." She paused again. "I'm 'on leave' from work—isn't that a charming way to say they don't want a lesbian murderess around? So, it doesn't really matter whether I sleep or not."

"Oh, Jody, I'm so sorry . . ." Meg, hardly knowing what to say, blundered on. "I don't know why I called . . . I guess I just wanted to tell you I really feel badly about what's happened to you. I mean, first, you had to deal with Susan's death . . . and now . . ." She stopped, flustered, not sure how to continue.

"Thanks, Meg." Jody's voice softened a little. "It's nice that you called. It's just that everything's been pulled out from under me and turned upside down. I was just beginning to deal with the death . . . I'd just gotten Susan's clothes packed up in boxes; they're in the bedroom now. I can't sleep in there. Does that sound nuts? I've been sleeping on the couch . . . or not sleeping . . . But you know what the hardest thing is?" Suddenly, the words were tumbling out. "My friends—I thought they were my friends—people that knew us think I did it. I feel like I'm going crazy."

"Jody . . ." Meg fumbled a moment and then blurted out, "Can I come over? I mean . . . you sure sound like you could use some company." Meg was blushing to her roots. Being so assertive was not her style.

"Oh, Meg, it's so late. Are you serious?"

Meg took heart from the hint of relief she heard in Jody's voice. "I could be there in half an hour. Hey, did you eat tonight?"

"I don't think so . . . I've been kind of losing track of stuff like that."

"I'll pick up a pizza. What do you like?"

"Anything except anchovies."

"You got it. See you soon."

15
First Visit with Jody

After she grabbed her windbreaker and wallet, Meg raced to the truck. Although she was nervous and apprehensive, she felt more alive than she had since the night Kim had broken up with her. Here she was, dashing off into the brightly star-lit night, flinging herself into another adventure. She almost shouted out loud with unexpected joy, life coursing again so strongly through her tingling body.

She was in such a hurry that she drove right by the pizza place, making an illegal U-turn when she discovered what she had done. Impatiently, she paced back and forth as the order was prepared, cursing for not thinking about calling ahead. Then, she was on her way again, the cab filling with the aroma of sausage and cheese.

Jody's cabin was set back from the road, the last of a series of what at one time must have been summer cottages, but now had the flavor of being lived-in all the time. There was no light but a dim flicker of firelight to guide Meg as she picked her way through the darkness. Gathering her courage to knock, the pizza balanced precariously on one hand, she glanced up, noticing the broken porch light. Well, that would explain the lack of a brighter welcome.

By the third knock, the door opened. Jody looked so tired and dishevelled it was all Meg could do not to drop the pizza right there and take her into her arms. Jody looked at Meg, a wan smile struggling for expression on a face that held too much sorrow. "Hi, Meg, I'm glad you're here. You certainly made good time."

Meg blushed, hoping it wouldn't be noticed in the darkened doorway. "I tend to drive pretty fast." She had no intention of telling Jody exactly *how* fast she had driven tonight. "Uh, . . ." Meg felt inarticulate, more like an adolescent boy than a competent, middle-aged dyke, "I hope you're hungry. I ordered an extra large."

"I must be. I don't think I've eaten since breakfast. Come on in. I have a fire going. I know it isn't that cold, but I just can't stand having the lights on. I feel too exposed." Meg was touched by her openness.

There were several cushions thrown in front of the fire. They sat down with the pizza between them, but Jody jumped right up. "I forgot the napkins. Do you want a Coke? I don't have any beer or wine in the house. After Susan died, I emptied them out and threw the bottles into the garbage."

"A Coke would be fine. I don't drink much myself—just an occasional glass of wine or a wine cooler." Meg found herself blathering. Was she trying to tell Jody that she didn't have a problem with alcohol, as Susan so obviously had had? What difference did it make anyway? She was just here on an errand of mercy, wasn't she?

When Jody came back, Meg decided to keep silent and just listen. After each had polished off a couple of pieces of pizza, Jody began to talk, haltingly at first.

"It's been over a month, and I still can't believe Susan's dead. I keep expecting her to come home, and each time I wake up I realize all over again that she died. Does that make me crazy or something?"

Meg knew that feeling well. It was just like when Kim had dumped her. It had taken her weeks—months—before her whole being, waking and sleeping, knew it. She looked Jody straight in the eye, surprised at her own boldness. "No, it's very normal. It may be a long time before it really sinks in."

Jody continued, her face showing more and more pain. "And when I'm awake I keep thinking of her being in the van and watching the water come up over her head and not being able to get out." Jody strated crying, her whole body shaking. "I keep going over it in my mind. Why couldn't I get her out? I tried, but I couldn't get her seatbelt unfastened. That was so stupid. She had wanted to drive home, but I wouldn't let her—she was really drunk. I was so mad at her, but I still made her fasten her seatbelt. I won't drive anywhere if people aren't belted up, and that was what killed her. Fine protector *I* am!"

Meg reached out, took Jody's hand and held on to it tightly. "Jody, it sounds to me as if you did everything you *could* do to get her out."

"Sometimes, I wish I had died, too. It couldn't be any worse than blaming myself for her death. And now everyone else blames me, too. I was questioned for hours this morning."

"Have they filed any charges?"

"No, but I have to be available for questioning, which means I can't leave the county."

"Do they know what your relationship to Susan really was?" Meg probed gently.

"Yeah," Jody replied bitterly. "It didn't take long for them to figure that out. You'd think they were each personally offended I was a lesbian. It doesn't take a psychic to read their minds: 'Boy, babe, sleep with me and I'll change your mind.'"

"Are the police questioning anyone else?"

Jody nodded. "Most of the women at the gathering. A lot of them are angry with me for 'exposing' them."

"Do the police have any suspects?"

"They're looking for Susan's ex-lover, Terry. She has a police record. She slugged a policeman at a gay rights demonstration in Boise when he suggested he could 'cure' her."

Meg laughed. "Well, I admire her guts if not her judgment. Do you think she had something to do with it?"

"No, not when it gets right down to it. Believe me, I have no fondness for Terry. When I met Susan, Terry was beating her, and they were both into drugs. I can't stand being around her. She was awfully mad when Susan decided to come back to Oregon with me." Jody paused for a moment. "But Terry's aggression was right out in the open. I can't imagine her doing something devious like cutting the brake cables."

"Well, if you don't think it was her, do you have any other ideas?"

Jody shrugged. "I keep asking myself that over and over again. Sure, we had our share of tiffs with friends but nothing that would lead to anything like that." Jody stopped, as if she had no more energy to keep going. She glanced over at Meg's drink, saw it was empty, then jumped up. "Here, let me get you another. I think I had better put the rest of the pizza back in the oven. It's getting too cold to eat."

Meg settled back, trying to marshal her thoughts. She heard Jody open the refrigerator door, then heard the bathroom door close. Just then the phone rang, shattering the stillness.

Meg picked it up. "Hello?" Silence. "Hello?" Meg's voice rose. "Hello? Who's there?"

A male voice finally spoke. "Hey, bull dyke. Can I come over and lick your pussy? Then maybe I can stick my—"

"No, thanks!" Feeling powerless and violated, Meg slammed the receiver down.

Jody called out from the kitchen. "Who was it?"

Meg, shaking, answered, "It was just an obscene call."

Jody sighed. "That makes eight so far today. The local male population seems to be enraged that a lesbian is living in their community. I even got one woman caller who called me a whore and an abomination to God."

"Oh, Jody." Meg, her voice full of softness, moved toward her, although she had no idea what she was going to do once she got there. "I'm so sorry. I don't know how you stand it."

Then, from outside the door came the sound of a car, driving much too fast up the gravel driveway. Just as Meg reached Jody, headlights glared through the window, brakes squealed, and the window exploded.

Meg grabbed Jody and hit the floor behind the table, narrowly missing the kitchen counter. Shards of glass showered the kitchen. They huddled under the tenuous protection of the table for a few moments, waiting to see if there was more to come. Then the car backed up, the engine revved, and it shot out as fast as it had come.

"That's it!" Meg spoke, with determination in her voice. "You're coming with me. It just isn't safe here anymore, especially at night. Get your night things and get into the truck."

Jody, in shock, moved mechanically to the bathroom to get her toothbrush. Meg, after getting up carefully and dusting the glass shards from her shirt, grabbed Jody's coat from the hanger in back of the front door, took Jody's arm, and slammed the door closed, making sure it was locked.

16
A Nest for Two

Stepping out into the threatening darkness, Meg put her left arm around Jody's shoulders. Jody was quiet, withdrawn, shrunk up into herself, so different from the woman Meg had met at the ocean just a few weeks before. It was as if Jody had lost something of herself.

Looking carefully in all directions, Meg led Jody to the truck, which had not been damaged by the recent attack. As they crossed the open space, Meg's blood started coursing with the spirit of her Amazon ancestors, women who fought bravely and made love tenderly. This was a time to fight. Maybe the lovemaking would come later.

After they got out on Highway 101, Meg felt safer, although she still drove as fast as she could. Jody kept silent next to her, huddled up against the far door. Meg, hesitating at first, finally reached out her right hand, squeezing Jody's knee reassuringly. It was no time to get hung up on her fear of touching other people. Tonight all the rules she had lived by were suspended. This was an emergency calling for different tactics.

They drove through the night in silence. A few minutes later, Meg turned off the road, happier than ever to see her little cabin. Her porch light cast a pale yellow glow onto the minuscule front yard, making Meg feel safe again, caressed by its faint light. She was determined this would be a real harbor for Jody, a place for her to sleep and rest and prepare for the battles to come.

Feeling very protective, Meg opened the cab door, stepping down with a firm tread. This was her territory, and Goddess have mercy on whoever tried to invade it. Jody didn't move, so Meg walked around to the passenger's side and opened the door. Jody, still in shock, moved sluggishly, but Meg knew how to handle that. In her years of ministry, she had been present with people during every imaginable kind of crisis. Her mind flashed back to the time she had been summoned to the deathbed of a young boy, looking so still and fragile against the stark white sheets, his mother keening over his body. Surely, what she had learned on nights like those would serve her in good stead here.

The night had taken on an unseasonal chill, the moist sea air coming in through a window that Meg had inadvertently left open. Meg strode across the room and closed it, then began to build up a roaring fire. When she had finished, she turned to face Jody, who was still standing near the front door. "How about some hot chocolate? I could sure use some."

Taking Jody's silence for assent, Meg began assembling the ingredients. After she took the chocolate and sugar down from the cupboard, she found just enough milk in the refrigerator for two large cups. She would have to drink her coffee black in the morning, but it was worth it. She mixed the ingredients, put them on low heat, then rummaged in the back of the cupboard, searching for the remnants of a package of miniature marshmallows. There was just a handful left, but that would be enough.

When the chocolate started simmering, she turned off the stove and removed the pan from the heat. Looking overhead, Meg glanced through her large collection of stone mugs. Finally, her gaze rested on one with a sailboat etched on its side. That was the one for Jody. A sailboat needed the wind in order to move. The sailor took the measure of the wind and set her sails accordingly to make it take her where she wanted. Jody needed help now to set her sails and begin moving into the wind again.

When she returned to the living room, Jody was sitting on the couch, staring into the fire, as if trying to read some secret there. "Here's your chocolate, Jody. Be careful. It's hot."

Jody looked up, the beginnings of a smile on her face, the lines around her eyes softening a bit. "Thanks. It looks good."

Meg sat down beside her, cradling her cup in her hands. It had a picture of a clown on it, a souvenir from a summer in Berkeley, where she had taken a class in clowning. As Toby the Tramp, she had learned to play the nose flute and make balloon animals. She liked clowns—they were clumsy and awkward, fumbling and falling in front of large crowds to get them to laugh after the tension produced by the high-wire acts and lion tamer. Through Toby, Meg had learned that it was all right to fail, all right to stumble all over her own big feet, as long as she did it with love.

Feeling a lot like Toby, a bit awkward but full of love, Meg turned to Jody. "You're safe now, Jody. No one knows you're here. You don't have to answer the phone or be afraid that someone will throw anything through the window. You can stay here as long as you like."

Jody answered in an uncharacteristically small, childlike voice. "God, I'm so tired. I just want to sleep until the nightmare is over."

Noticing Jody's cup was empty, Meg reached out and placed it on the rug. "I have only one bedroom. Why don't you sleep there? I can sleep on the sofa next to the fire."

"No, I'm not going to roust you out of your own bed. I'll be fine here. Anyway, I've gotten used to sleeping on couches lately."

It seemed best not to argue. "Okay, let me get you a comforter and build up the fire." Meg threw two more large logs on the fire, then fetched the comforter from her own bed. Her electric blanket would keep her warm.

"Here you are, Jody. Is there anything else you need?"

"No thanks, Meg. I just want to sleep." Her head was already on a cushion she had picked up from the floor. It was all Meg could do not to lie down next to her, hold her in her arms and dare the world to try to hurt her anymore.

Not wanting the evening to end, Meg went into her own room reluctantly, leaving the door ajar so that she could listen, the way she used to do when her kids were small and needed her in the night. She lay still for a long time, listening to the sounds of Jody's breathing, not letting herself go until she was sure Jody was asleep. Finally, when she heard the slow, deep breathing coming from the other room, Meg fell into a restless sleep.

She had no idea how long she had slept when she sat up in bed, startled. As she aroused herself, she heard cries from the living room, "Help me! I'm drowning!" It was Jody! She must be having a nightmare. Flinging off the covers, Meg was at her side in a moment. "Jody! It's all right. You're just having a bad dream." Meg put out her hand and touched Jody's shoulder gently, the way she had soothed her own children so many times in the past.

"God, where am I?" Her voice was panicky.

"It's all right. You're at my house. You were having a bad dream, but you're safe now."

Every time I go to sleep I see us going over the edge of the parking lot into the water. I start choking and panicking and never know if I'm going to get out alive. Every night, Susan dies again in front of my eyes, and I wake up and I'm alone, and I know the dream is real." Jody's breathing was jagged and gasping, her pulse was racing, and sweat had broken out on her forehead.

"It's all right, it's all right," Meg kept repeating like a mantra, hoping her voice would wrap Jody in its warmth and peace. "It's still night. Why don't you try to go back to sleep?"

Jody's eyes were beseeching. "I just can't. I don't want to have that dream again. I'm afraid."

Meg moved closer and took her in her arms and held her tight. She began rocking instinctively, stroking Jody's tense back and murmuring in her ear. She could feel Jody's body begin to relax. Jody seemed to melt into her as the rocking continued rhythmically.

"Come with me," Meg declared, her voice brooking no opposition. "It's cold in here. I'm going to put you in my bed and hold you until you go to sleep. I'll keep the monsters away from you." Meg smiled in the darkness, remembering other nights with other monsters. "I have three children who can give you references."

Jody looked up, childlike trust on her face. Meg took her by the hand and led her into her room, sat her on the bed and took off Jody's jeans. "You can sleep in your underwear and T-shirt. You'll be more comfortable."

Meg went around to the other side of the bed, sat down, reached across to Jody, still sitting on the edge, and drew her down to her. She pulled Jody to herself, put Jody's head in the crook of her arm, and held her gently but firmly. It was strange. Meg had had a lot of sexual fantasies about Jody in the last few weeks, but now all she felt was an overwhelming and fierce tenderness and protectiveness. Jody, sensing she was safe, was soon asleep in Meg's arms.

Meg just held her, watchful, admiring the way the moonbeams danced on her face, highlighting her blond hair. Towards dawn, Meg, too, feel asleep, still cradling Jody in her arms.

17
Jody Is Arrested

Around 8:30, Meg, feeling Jody stirring, opened her eyes. She had thought when Kim had broken up with her that she would never again hold another woman in her arms. It was nice to be wrong.

Softly, Meg whispered, "Good morning, Jody. Looks like you got some sleep."

Jody, whose back was pressed up against Meg's breasts, turned over as Meg reluctantly released her grasp. Jody sighed, stretching like a cat in the morning sun. "This is the first night I have really slept since Susan . . ." She left the rest of the sentence unspoken, but the image filled both their minds.

"I'm glad," Meg said, trying to think of something more meaningful to say. But what exactly *did* one say to a woman who had just spent the night in your arms, a woman who was not your lover? Getting such a late start in lesbian life was sometimes a disadvantage.

Jody, too, seemed a little awkward. "Uh, thanks for holding me last night." She laughed gently. "Ordinarily, I don't go to bed with a woman on our first date."

Embarrassed, Meg laughed. "How about some breakfast?" she asked in a hearty voice she detested as soon as she heard it.

"I don't know," Jody replied hesitantly. "I should be getting back to the cabin."

"It's still early. Why don't I make us something, then I can drive you home."

"Well, if you twist my arm."

"I have several specialties—blueberry pancakes, walnut waffles, French toast . . ."

"How about blueberry pancakes? They're my favorite."

"Sure. With bacon or sausage?" Meg had been hoarding the last of the bacon for rice pilaf, but this was more important.

"Bacon would be good."

"Great!" Meg answered with gusto, certain of her role as hostess and cook. Within minutes, the bacon was sizzling, the syrup and butter were out, the batter was mixed, and the coffee was boiling.

"How about some fresh coffee? I'm afraid we used up all the milk last night."

"Black is fine."

Meg found that it was fine with her too, although before today she would have told anyone that she hated her coffee black. Breakfast passed quickly, each comfortable in the other's presence. Neither brought up the events of the past night, so the conversation was mostly about the weather and food, with long periods of companionable silence.

"Well," Jody said with reluctance, after she had polished off a fourth pancake, "I guess I had better go home and see if the house is still there."

Meg sighed, hoping the morning would never end. "Why don't I drive you now? I can clean up the kitchen later."

It was a beautiful summer morning, the sun dancing on the waves, the seagulls swooping high overhead. It was tempting to just keep driving down the coast, fleeing Jody's troubles, but Meg dutifully swung into the road leading to Jody's house. Both were apprehensive about what they might find, but there seemed to be no further damage. "Do you want me to stay and help you clean up?" Meg offered.

"No," said Jody, the cab door already open. "I think I need a little time by myself. I need to work out some things." Jody paused. "I don't know how to thank you for being there for me last night, Meg. I'm glad I asked you to come over. I don't think I could have gotten through another night alone, especially here."

Meg didn't want to go, but Jody was firm. "Okay, but if you need anything—anything at all—please call me. Here's my number."

She scribbled her number on a piece of paper lying on the floor of the truck. "Don't lose it. I'll call you tonight. If you don't want to answer the phone, I'll call once and let it ring twice, then call right back. That way you'll know that it's me, and," Meg added, hesitation in her voice, "you're welcome to spend the nights at my place as long as you need to."

"Thanks, I may need to take you up on that," said Jody, waving as Meg left.

Back at her own cabin, Meg felt bereft. Everywhere she looked she could feel Jody's presence, as if it had taken over the space and filled it with new possibilities. Trying to block out her loneliness, she tried to do some writing.

Once a month, Meg wrote a sermon for a Catholic news service, a job left over from her days in Catholic ministry. She really needed the $125 a month the job brought in, but it was harder and harder to write something that would "fly" in a Catholic church on Sunday morning.

Looking back, Meg could hardly believe how long she had been part of such a patriarchal institution. She had swallowed hook, line, and sinker all the lies about a male God, a male Savior and male-only priests. Only when she found her own power and worth as a woman did she start to throw up all the toxins whose traces were still in her system. Still uncertain where her new spirituality would take her, she knew it would be healing, whole and woman-centered.

But try as she might, Meg couldn't concentrate, so she poured herself a cup of coffee, no longer as appealing without milk as it had been when Jody was there, and sat out on the back stoop for awhile. As the mid-morning breeze played with her hair, her mind started wandering. There wasn't much point wasting time wondering if Jody was ready for another involvement. That was sheer guesswork at this point. But when Meg's thoughts strayed to Kim, her first lover, she felt she had some unfinished business with her. True, they hadn't communicated at all in the last several months, but Meg still thought of her, still had to keep herself sometimes from dialing her number.

It was time to do something about that. Meg got up, putting her partially drunk cup of coffee on the step, and went into the cabin. She opened the hall closet and quickly found the box she was looking for, the one filled with relics of her first love affair, not yet quite dead. Picking it up, she went back into the living room and took out each item one by one. As she glanced over them, the memories of a time so near, yet so far, came back in full force. There was the bottle of Welch's grape juice, still unopened. It was to have been used in a Eucharist they never shared together. Next to it lay a sheaf of wheat, never to be ground into flour for bread, a poignant reminder of their abortive and violent parting.

Under them lay three fat candles which they had lit the first time they had made love: green for life, purple for their women's love, white for purity. Meg had never had the heart to light them again or the heartlessness to throw them away. Lying next to them were two wooden plaques Kim had made and given to Meg, with sayings from e.e. cummings: "Love is a place/Thru this place/of Love, Move!" and "Yes is a World,/And in this World/of Yes, Live!" But ultimately, Kim hadn't been able to say yes to new possibilities of life.

Putting them aside, Meg reached again into the box containing pieces of a life that had never really happened. She grasped a small wooden plaque with a picture of an Indian mother carrying her child in a sling on her back, a picture Meg had glued on to her dashboard to become her guardian angel. At the time, she had felt so safe and loved by Kim, certain she would be sheltered like a child in her mother's arms. How wrong she had been. The day after Kim had broken up with her, Meg had wrenched it off in anger, leaving a permanent mark on the dashboard of the truck.

Then there was the picture album, which Meg, in one of her more optimistic moods, had labelled "Our Story." It was filled with furtive, stolen moments carved out from the rest of their lives: a two-week trip to Berkeley to study together, a fast trip to Salt Lake City, a weekend camping trip, a trip to a guest resort. Meg had been living at home with her husband, and Kim had been living with Cheryl, while declaring to Meg that she was waiting for just the right moment to leave. Enough pieces of living to fill one lonely scrapbook—aptly named, for it really was just scraps left over from their other lives. There weren't enough remnants to piece together a whole life with each other.

She had almost reached the bottom of the box when she came across a turquoise and silver ring tangled up in a piece of green yarn. Perhaps, this was the most painful memento of all. Kim had given it to Meg along with a card which had said, "To my honey." Meg put it on one last time, then tucked it into a corner of the box.

The green yarn was a particularly painful memory. Meg remembered picking it up off the floor with the other wrappings after Kim's grandson had flung it aside after opening his birthday present. After Kim and Meg had returned from San Francisco, Meg and Kim had untangled it that night in their apartment in Berkeley, then woven it together into a green triangle, which they had hung over their bed. It had been as if they were finally beginning to untangle their past lives and reweave their lives together. However, when it came time for Kim to move out and begin her new life with Meg, it proved easier to untangle a piece of yarn than her life with Cheryl.

The last item was a bottle of massage oil. They had always used it when they made love, anointing each other with gentle caresses. She still remembered the way her hand had felt after making love and the sweet smell of oil, mixed with the pungent odor of sex. God, it still hurt to remember the feel of Kim's sure hands on her body, knowing they would never touch her again.

The phone rang, jarring her out of her deepening reverie. Reluctantly, Meg got up, placing the oil back on her coffee table.

"Hello?"

"God, Meg, I'm glad you're home!"

Meg immediately recognized Jody's voice, her panicky tone jolting Meg back to the present.

"You sound awful! What's the matter?" Meg queried with concern in her voice.

"I've been brought in again for questioning. I'm being held this time. They haven't pressed formal charges yet, but I told them I'm not going to say anything more until I have a lawyer. I'm scared, Meg. Do you know anyone you can call for me? I've never needed a lawyer before."

Meg racked her memory, and a name came up. "Yeah, I do. I know a woman lawyer in Portland who's politically active in the lesbian community. Why don't I call her? Then, I'll come down to the jail. I don't want you to be there all by yourself."

Jody sounded relieved. "Thanks, Meg. They're all looking at me like I'm a freak. I don't know when they're going to let me out."

"Okay, just hang on. I'll put in a call to my friend and be there within a half hour."

As soon as she hung up, Meg made her call. Fortunately, her friend Marty was in her office. Meg explained the situation as clearly as she could.

Marty listened carefully, asking an occasional question. "This sounds big. I think I had better come down and deal with this directly. It'll take me a couple of hours. Why don't I meet you at the jail?"

"Okay. I'm on my way." Meg's voice filled with relief. "And thanks. See you soon." In minutes, Meg was in the truck, heading towards the police station, wondering what she would say when she got there. Well, she hoped something would come to mind. She just kept telling herself she had to keep focused on Jody and not worry about herself.

18
To The Rescue

Meg was glad she didn't see any highway patrolmen on her way to the jail. She broke every law she thought she could get away with, including running a red light. When she got to the police station, there was only one space left in the parking lot, a tight one right next to the drainage ditch. Squeezing in as close as she could to the car to her right, she pulled the emergency brake without thought, even though she knew it didn't work, and opened the door cautiously. She had to hold onto the door handle to keep herself from falling into the ditch when she got out. Nonetheless, she still got her shoes muddy, then slipped and got her knee dirty.

Dusting herself off as best she could, Meg moved warily towards the front door. She realized she really must look the part of a dyke and that she would be under the suspicious and disapproving gaze of the entire police department, but there was no help for it. Jody needed her, and that was all that mattered. As she pushed open the glass door, Meg mumbled to herself, "I'm a law-abiding citizen, just like anyone else. I deserve the same attention and respect as anyone else who walks through this door." She almost believed it.

She approached the front desk. Her courage wavered as she waited for the matron on duty to lift her eyes from the police blotter in front of her. "Er, excuse me, but I need some help," she managed to blurt out.

The policewoman raised her eyes grudgingly, taking Meg in with one disapproving glance. "Yes," she said perfunctorily, "can I help you?"

"Ah . . . yes, I'm here to see Jody Miller."

"What makes you think she's here?"

"She called me from here a few minutes ago." Meg's jaw tensed.

"Are you her lawyer?" The woman's voice held a mixture of doubt and scorn.

Meg stood firm. "Well, no, I'm a friend. Her lawyer won't be here for a couple more hours."

"I'm sorry, but you can't see her. She's being questioned."

Meg persisted. "How long will that take."

"I have no idea. It could take several hours, even if she isn't formally charged."

"I'm sorry, but . . ." Meg swallowed. "I have no intention of leaving until I see her."

"Suit yourself. It's a free country." The woman returned to her work.

Meg looked around the bleak reception area, obviously not designed for comfort. She settled on a black metal chair next to the front door, a drooping potted plant standing sentinel next to it. Well, it was better than nothing, and this way she could see if Jody came out, while keeping an eye out for Marty's arrival.

The clock said 2:10. Was it only a few hours ago that she had held Jody in her arms, thinking that she somehow had the power to take away her pain and protect her from harm? How foolish! All Meg could do was sit there impotently and wait.

Glancing again at the clock, Meg saw that it was only 2:15. It was going to be a long vigil. Not having had the time or inclination to bring a book, Meg looked through the magazines on the coffee table next to her. All she found were old copies of *Outdoor Life* and *Sports Illustrated*. It took her only a few moments to confirm what she had always suspected: these magazines were boring.

Next, she tried shutting her eyes and counting to 60, seeing how close she could come to a clock minute. Her first attempt was 56 seconds, her second 61. That took care of a few more minutes. The clock face, the hour hand on two, the minute hand on six, taunted her, daring her to try to ignore it or make it go faster.

This was ridiculous. She was beginning to think the clock was stuck, that she was in some sort of hellish time warp where minutes lasted for days. So Meg decided to relive the night with Jody, minute by minute. As she recreated the events of the previous hours, Meg's body began to slow down, her muscles relaxed, her breathing became deeper and more rhythmic. Soon, she could actually feel Jody in her arms again, and this time she held her even more closely, sending out a white light to protect the two of them. Time seemed to stand still, defeated, its power over her broken by the clear, focused love she poured forth. Everything seemed to drop away, footsteps fading, phones muted. "It's all right, Jody. Be strong." Over and over again, Meg repeated her mantra, rocking back and forth in rhythm with the softly whispered words.

"Meg? Are you asleep?" A firm hand shook her shoulder.

Meg felt groggy, as if she had been asleep, although it had really been more like she'd been in a self-induced trance. Her tongue felt thick and unwieldy, as if she were under a deep anaesthetic. With great effort, she forced her eyes open and tried to remember how to speak. "Oh, hi, Marty. You made good time," she finally managed.

"What do you mean? It's almost 5:30. I got tied up in an accident on I-5 near Terwilliger Boulevard."

Meg was really confused now. It couldn't be much after three, could it? She looked up at the clock over the front desk, and sure enough, it said 5:33. She had been sitting in the chair for over three hours without moving.

She shook her head, trying to dispel the fogginess she felt. "No, I wasn't asleep. It's great to see you."

Marty's freckled face, short red hair, and almost six-foot height reminded Meg of an Amazon warrior, whose weapon was the law, not a sword. She was wearing what were for her conservative clothing: a russet silk print blouse, corduroy jacket and matching pants, sensible walking shoes, with a bulging briefcase in her left hand. She must have come straight from a court appearance.

"So, tell me what's going on." Marty spoke brusquely, all business now. "Has she been charged with anything?"

"I honestly don't know. The woman at the front desk wouldn't tell me anything."

"Okay. Wait here. I'll find out." As Marty strode to the desk, Meg wished her luck, not doubting for a moment that Marty would get what she wanted. Within minutes, Marty was back.

"They're still questioning her, but haven't filed any charges—yet. If they haven't done that by tomorrow, I will file a writ of habeas corpus. That should force their hand."

"You mean they can keep her here all night?" Meg's voice was edged with desperation.

"Unfortunately, yes. We can't do anything until morning. I had a message sent to her that her lawyer was here and not to answer any more questions until I come back in the morning. I think we could all use a night off."

"Damn them! This is so stupid. I know she didn't kill Susan." Meg was on the brink of doing something violent, although she knew it really wouldn't help. She grasped the arms of the chair until her knuckles turned white.

"Come on, Meg. There's nothing we can do tonight. We'll be down here first thing in the morning." Marty sounded so reasonable and logical.

"You're probably right, but I hate leaving her here all alone."

"She's not alone," Marty reassured her. "She's got you for a friend and me for a lawyer. What more could any woman want?" Marty smiled, coaxing a weak response from Meg.

"Okay, you've convinced me. Look, why don't you come over to my place? You can spend the night there, and I can fill you in on the situation."

"You're on. Why don't I follow you in my truck? I don't want to leave it here. I have a feeling some officers in this town might be allergic to my bumper stickers."

"Sounds good to me." Meg led the way. "My truck is parked over there in back of that van."

As they rounded the corner of the van, Meg gasped. Her truck had rolled into the ditch, its left front tire buried up to the hubcap in mud, the cab at a crazy angle. "God, this is all I need! I guess I'll have to call the Auto Club. There's no way I can drive out of there by myself."

"Wait a minute. Don't be too hasty. I have a chain in the back of my pickup. Why don't we rescue it ourselves?"

"Why not? Two dykes together should be able to pull a truck out of a ditch." As Meg helped Marty hook the chain to her rear bumper, her confidence came flooding back. Yes, she could be there for Jody. No, she wasn't a failure. She had done all she could for her and would keep on it until Jody was free. As the chain between the two vehicles tightened, her own fell away, and with a jerk from Marty's truck freeing hers, Meg felt strong and light again.

She realized she'd been in such a hurry when she got to the police station that she had pulled the emergency brake without remembering it was broken and had forgotten to put her tire against a curb. It didn't take long for the truck to roll down the gentle slope until the drainage ditch pulled it in. Meg backed up, signalling to Marty. "Marty, the emergency brake is shot. I guess it's time to get it fixed. Could you follow me to the gas station so I can drop it off tonight? Maybe they can get it fixed by tomorrow."

"Sure, no problem. Let's go."

It didn't take long to talk to the attendant. He assured her that the brake would be fixed by mid-morning, so Marty and Meg continued on in Marty's 4-wheeler.

19
More Sabotage

Both Meg and Marty were up soon after dawn. Marty had slept comfortably enough on the couch, but Meg didn't feel like cooking so they went to Sambo's for pancakes and sausage. A few minutes before nine, they left to make sure they would be at the police station on time. As they drove by the gas station where Meg had left her truck, she could see it parked in the back; she assumed that meant it had been fixed. Maybe they could pick it up later, but first they had to see Jody.

This time, there was plenty of room in the parking lot. Meg reclaimed the black chair, while Marty approached the desk. In a few minutes, she disappeared with the police matron; Meg assumed she was being escorted to see Jody. How she wished she were going with her! In less than ten minutes, Marty returned, her face gloomy and drawn. "Well, Meg, it looks pretty bad right now. They've decided to charge Jody with first-degree murder. Her arraignment is at ten this morning."

"What? I can't believe it! Why do they think it was her?" Meg was dumbfounded.

Marty tried to sound reassuring. "It's pretty standard procedure to thoroughly investigate the one closest to the victim. They claim they're still checking into other leads."

"How's Jody doing? Do you think the judge will let her out on bail?"

"I don't know. I'll go with her to her arraignment in an hour. I will ask the judge to release her on her own recognizance, based on her length of stay in the community and her work record. We'll try that first and see where it goes."

"Will they let me see her?"

"Not yet. Let's wait until we know more. If she doesn't get released right away, I'll make sure you're on her approved visitor list."

"Look, Marty, I'm not sure I can sit still for the next hour. How about driving me to the gas station and retrieving my truck with me?"

"Sounds like a good idea. Let's go." Marty led the way to her truck, and soon they were at the gas station. Meg was relieved that the young attendant wasn't on duty. There was an older man working on a car who could help her. Marty parked, then Meg walked over to the man.

"Excuse me, I left my truck here last night. It had a faulty emergency brake. Is it ready yet?"

The man stood up, wiping his grease-stained hands on an oil-soaked rag he kept in his back pocket. "Yes. Come on into the office with me. I fixed it myself early this morning." He had the bill right on the desk top. "That will be $15.82."

Well, that was more than she had on her or in the bank, so Meg grudgingly took out one of her two credit cards and proffered it. She owed $243 on that one and was trying to bring down the balance each month, obviously a lost cause. The other one she kept for life-or-death emergencies, with the entire $2,500 credit limit untouched. It had originally been hers and Mark's, but she had kept it when they separated, feeling no need to inform the credit card company of her new status— or lack of it. Meg knew some of her more politically correct lesbian acquaintances would condemn her for retaining some vestige of heterosexist privilege, but she had no intention of telling them. As the man ran it through the card machine, Meg asked, "Was it frayed or disconnected or what?"

"Well, it looks real frayed, but it's been cut too, cut all the way through," the man replied thoughtfully.

"What? That just doen't make sense. I looked at it myself when it first gave out a few months ago and didn't spot anything like that." Meg sounded confused. "I'm not a mechanic, but I *know* I could spot something obvious like a cut cable."

"Well, maybe," the man sounded skeptical, "but it would still be a good idea for you to get your hood latch fixed as soon as you can. There are just too many crazies in the world for you to have your engine and wiring accessible to anyone who wants to cause damage."

"You have a point, but I think it'll have to wait until next month." Meg signed the receipt, thanked him, and walked slowly to the truck, turning over all sorts of possibilities in her mind. Halfway there, she wheeled around, returning to the office. "Oh, can I have the cable you took out?"

"Sure, it's right here in a plastic bag, with a tag with your license number on it."

"Thanks again." Holding the bag in her hand as if it were a poisonous snake, Meg walked back to the truck. "It's fixed, Marty. Why don't we go on back to the police station now? Maybe I can see Jody when they bring her out for her arraignment. I'll follow in my truck."

"Okay. Meet you there."

When she got into the cab, Meg carefully placed the cable in the back of the truck, her mind still spinning. As Meg followed Marty, she kept going at the problem. Who could have done it? When had it happened? Was it mere coincidence that the police were claiming Jody's van had also had the same thing done to it? Or were the two events somehow connected?

It was 9:42 when they got back to the police station. A few minutes later, Jody came out, accompanied by an armed police matron. She was dressed in a blue denim dress and plastic sandals. Her feet were shackled together, making her shuffle unnaturally as she tried to keep her footing. Her hands were chained together in front, with the chain going around her waist.

When she saw Jody, Meg drew back as if she had been slapped. Fortunately, Jody hadn't seen her right away, so by the time she glanced over, Meg had on what she hoped was her brave and optimistic face. She smiled at Jody, trying in that look to pour all of her love and strength into her. Jody smiled back, the fingers of her left hand waving as much as the chains would allow.

"Okay," said Marty, much more used to the legal formalities than Meg, "let's get over to the courtroom and see if we can get her out of this place."

Shocked by Jody's appearance, Meg had trouble getting up and walking, but her feet somehow managed to remember to put themselves one in front of the other.

The courtroom was empty, except for the stenographer and court clerk. Marty went up to the defense table, with Meg in the front row right behind her. In less than a minute, Jody, still guarded by the matrons, entered from a side door. At the back of the courtroom was a policeman, also armed. My God, what did they think Jody was going to do? Just then the back door opened, admitting two middle-aged men in business suits, looking strangely like reporters.

"All rise. The honorable Harry P. Johnson presiding." An older man, with a trim mustache and balding head, entered, walking as if long accustomed to power. Soon Marty stood up to state her case. "Your honor, we request that Ms. Miller be released on her own recognizance. She has no prior arrests or convictions of any kind. She is a responsible citizen in the community and has an excellent work record. She presents no threat to the welfare of the community, and there is no reason to believe that she will not be available for trial."

Then the district attorney, a young man obviously on his way up, stood to counter what Marty had said. "Your honor, Ms. Miller is accused of murdering Susan Callahan. If convicted of first-degree murder, she may receive the death penalty. I have no reason to think that she wouldn't take off if given the opportunity. I respectfully ask the court to keep her incarcerated until trial."

"Thank you, Mr. Schaefer. I hear your concern, but the trial date will be several months away in a capital case. I cannot see keeping her incarcerated for that long. I will, however, set the bail at $50,000, since this is such a serious matter. A court date will be set next week." Picking up his gavel, he hit it once on the desk. "This court is adjourned until 9:00 tomorrow morning."

"All rise," the clerk said. As the judge disappeared into his chambers, Jody and Marty hurriedly conferred before the matron led Jody back off to the jail. Meg couldn't even summon the will to move. It was as if all the bones had been sucked out of her body; Marty came around the railing. "It isn't as bad as all that, Meg."

"What do you mean?" Meg's voice was nearing hysteria. "Do you think Jody has $50,000 stashed away in a savings account? Or maybe," Meg's voice took on a note of bitterness, "you think I can save it out of my job as a motel maid?"

"Meg, calm down. You only have to put up ten percent for a bail bondsman. That is only $5,000. Jody has around $4,000 in savings, so we're talking a little over a thousand."

"Well, how are we going to raise even that much? Come on, Marty, this isn't a bunch of lesbian yuppies down here on the coast. Most of us are living on a shoestring. And even if we could, she's on unpaid leave of absence from her job for who knows how long."

"Well, we had better brainstorm. I know you don't want her sitting in jail for three or four months, maybe even half a year."

Suddenly, Meg had a thought. "Look, I *do* have credit on a credit card I keep for emergencies. I'm willing to use that."

Marty sounded hesitant. "Are you sure? That's a lot of money. I know you're just making it yourself. Do you really know Jody well enough to risk that?"

"Oh, come on, Marty. You really don't think Jody's going to take off, do you? Anyway, I have three jobs going right now: my writing, and my two jobs at the motel as maid and painter. Plus, you know I don't even have to pay rent. I'm willing to risk it.

"So, what are we waiting for?" Meg's voice sounded alive again. "Let's go the bank, and I'll get some instant cash and have them issue me a cashier's check. I don't want her here any longer than she has to be."

Within the hour, they were back, Meg clutching a $1,000 check tightly in her hand. The other thousand she had borrowed could go towards living expenses. She was going to get Jody to stay with her for awhile, despite the fact that she could barely make ends meet just for herself, let alone another. But it was worth all of it, even if she never got a penny back.

By noon, Jody was out the door, back in the clothes of the morning before, and out of that awful jail dress. Meg was suddenly shy and tongue-tied, but there was no need for words. Jody walked over to her, relief lighting up her face. Meg embraced her briefly and awkwardly, acutely aware of the oppressive surroundings.

Marty broke in. "Come on, let's get out of here." Her words galvanized them. When they got to the front door, they saw a group of reporters and a handful of the curious on the steps.

Marty took control. "Meg, go out the side door, circle around, and take my truck around to the back. We'll meet you there in two minutes. Hurry!" A few minutes later, the three of them, jammed together in the cab of the truck, were bouncing along a back road, hoping to elude overly inquisitive reporters. Jody clutched Meg's hand while she stared, rapt, out the window. "The greens are so green . . . you can't imagine what it's like to be locked up for 24 hours . . . it was the longest 24 hours of my life."

Marty, too, was staring out the window. "If you don't want to repeat it, let's get back to Meg's and start on your defense right now."

20
Fitting the Pieces Together

Meg's heart skipped a beat when she saw her little cabin, last refuge from a storm that was trying to sweep Jody away. As soon as they were inside, Meg felt safe again, and this time her hug expressed her tenderness. "I was so scared for you. It tore me apart when I saw you in chains."

"Well, it's going to be right up there with my least favorite memories." Jody's body still felt like it was bound.

"It's all right, Jody. You're safe here. You can relax."

"I feel so dirty and violated. I keep rubbing my wrists to keep the chains from chafing and pulling down my T-shirt because I think I'm still wearing that horrible blue prison dress."

Meg was relieved she wasn't the cause of Jody's tension. "Why don't you take a bath? I can lend you some clean clothes. While you're in the bathroom, I'll make some sandwiches and coffee."

"Sounds wonderful."

As Jody disappeared into the bathroom, Meg turned to Marty. "Marty, you know, don't you, that she couldn't have killed Susan?"

Marty lifted an eyebrow. "You sound like her lover. Are you?"

"God, Marty, . . . what a thing to say. Her lover just died. I'm just a friend."

"Sure." Her look was skeptical, but she was soon distracted by the business at hand. "When Jody gets out of the shower, we're going to sit down and figure out how to prove she didn't do it."

"I'd better get some food on, then. It's going to be a long session." It felt good to have something practical to do. Meg put on some coffee, then rummaged around in her cupboards and refrigerator to find something to feed her guests. There had been no time to replace the milk Jody had used up two nights before, but Marty also drank her coffee black. She managed to find a newly opened package of crackers, some cheese and pickles. A lone can of devilled ham mixed with mayonnaise and mustard would have to serve as a topping. Three sliced golden delicious apples, carrots and celery looked elegant on her vegetable dish. As an afterthought, Meg took what was left of a batch of chocolate chip cookie dough and started baking it.

Just as the aroma of melting chocolate and brown sugar began to fill the house, Jody came out of the bathroom, looking fresh, relaxed and ready to begin fighting for her life. The blue in her shirt highlighted her eyes; her blond hair was still damp. Meg had never seen anyone so beautiful or desirable.

Meg and Jody sat on the couch, a little apart; Marty sat on the chair opposite, a yellow legal pad on her lap. The food was spread out on the coffee table between them.

"I'll start," said Marty. "The case they have so far is circumstantial. They can show your involvement with Susan, your fight, your being at the scene of the crime. They have no other real suspects, especially if they can't locate Terry."

Meg interrupted. "Do you think they're going to go ahead and try Jody with just that? It sounds pretty weak."

"My guess is that, unless something else more promising jumps up and hits them in the face, they're going to put all of their energy into proving Jody did it."

Jody shook her head. "It seems to me they have a pretty weak case. Anyone could have cut those cables. The van was in that lot most of the day, and there were literally hundreds of people in the park that day, in addition to our group."

"That's true, Jody, but you're the one they have," Marty countered. "Plus, how could anyone have opened your hood?"

"Well, that's easy. Usually, I keep the cab locked, but that Saturday I found Susan in the van drinking, and I was furious. I pulled her out of the cab and slammed the door. I didn't even think about locking it . . . just getting her away from her booze. The problem is I can't prove it. But just supposing I did want to kill Susan, do you think I couldn't have arranged an accident like that by releasing the emergency brake manually instead of cutting the cables and making it seem suspicious?"

Marty thought for a moment. "That's a point, but it could be turned around against you. If you knew you were going to be the chief suspect, you might very well have cut the cables to throw suspicion on someone else."

Jody looked crestfallen. "I guess you're right. It feels to me like there's a lynch mob out there. I don't see how I'm going to get a fair trial in Lincoln County."

"That pretty much sums it up, Jody. Ever since the AIDS scare, the public is scared to death of queers, and they're not making any distinctions between gay men and lesbians. Measure 8 is just the tip of the iceberg. Have you read the arguments in favor of passage in the voter's pamphlet?"

Meg broke in. "I got it a couple of days ago, but I haven't had time to read it yet. It's here . . . somewhere . . ." She rummaged through a pile on the coffee table. "Ah!" She pulled it out and passed it to Marty.

Marty flipped it open to Measure 8. "Oh, here's a good one. They say that if Goldschmit's executive order keeping gay people from getting fired from the executive branch of the government solely because of their sexual orientation stands, 'what would prevent legislation to get special privileges for persons who prefer children as their sexual partners or animals or who knows what else?'"

Meg was enraged. "What do they mean, 'who knows what else?' What else is there? Dead people, ghosts . . . ?"

Marty answered thoughtfully. "Meg, it doesn't do any good to apply logic, common sense or your own experience to this. It's hatred and fear all rolled up into a poisonous little pill that they may very well be able to shove down people's throats." Marty continued to flip through the pamphlet. "Here are some 'facts' you might not be aware of. 'One study indicates that homosexual men ingest, on average, the fecal material of 23 different men per year. Another study, published in the American Journal of Public Health, demonstrated that of the homosexuals in the study, 5% drank urine, 7% incorporated a fist up their rectum, 53% swallowed semen and 59% received sperm up their rectum in the previous month.' Oh, here's a good one, probably the root of most of their fears: 'Other protected rights are not age-limited. That is, homosexual activity between an adult and a child, even if by consent, is a criminal offense. Such a contradiction cannot be tolerated in a protected right."

Jody protested, "That's crazy! Heterosexuals have a protected right to have their sexual orientation and sexual activity sanctioned by the state and by the constitution, but that doesn't mean that they are allowed to have sex with children!"

Marty's voice became pedantic. "Listen to me. I'm only going to say it once again: this whole thing is neither logical nor fair. So don't waste your breath using those yardsticks for their arguments. The latest polls show the yeses and noes pretty evenly divided."

"Even so, I'm not a gay man. Most of that doesn't apply to me," Jody said in a soft voice, trying to slip in one more argument.

"That doesn't matter. You're still homosexual, so you get the burden of both sexes. It doesn't matter that lesbians are the safest sex group in the country, next to sexual celibates. The general public still sees us tainted with the AIDS scare, and the fundies think it's only a matter of time before God's judgment descends on us, too."

"So, where does that leave us?" Meg asked.

"We have to take into account the political climate during this trial. Everyone is going to be out for your head, Jody. It will help them prove to the public that they are right about gays being dangerous and unstable."

"So, where does that leave our defense?" Meg continued, using the word 'our' unthinkingly and naturally.

"Their case is pretty weak, and I doubt that any more hard evidence is going to show up, but I have just so many challenges when juror selection comes up, and it's quite likely that you'll have a hostile jury, no matter how careful we are."

"You're saying I may be convicted because of people's prejudices, even if I'm not guilty."

"That's a real possibility, Jody. And even if you're found not guilty because of insufficient evidence, you're going to have the stigma for the rest of your life. People are just going to assume that you did it, but it couldn't be proven in a court of law."

Jody and Meg looked at each other hopelessly. Then Meg turned to Marty. "Well, it looks like the only way this is going to get cleared up is if we figure out who really did it and present them with the correct murderer."

"How can we do what the police haven't been able to do?" Jody questioned.

Meg forged ahead. "Jody, don't you see? We have an advantage. We *know* you didn't do it. That puts us ahead, and we can investigate other possibilities."

Marty nodded. "It's probably our best shot at this point. Let's go for it."

"Where do we start?" Jody and Meg spoke simultaneously.

Tearing off a page from her legal pad, Marty handed it to them, along with her pen. "Write down all the names of the women you saw that day at the beach." List complete, they mulled over each name and slowly, with a mixture of relief and frustration, crossed off the names one by one. By then, it was late afternoon, the sun shining in their eyes, cookie crumbs scattered over the furniture and their clothes.

"God, I'm so tired, I just want to sleep." Jody threw her pencil across the table and flung her head back against the couch.

Meg pleaded with her. "Just one more time, Jody. This time just relax and start from the top, from the time you heard about the party until the accident."

But Jody, eyes closed, just shook her head back and forth. Marty sighed. "Maybe we're all just too tired to think straight."

Jody ran her hand through her hair and looked from Marty to Meg with bleary eyes. "Look, . . . you've been great. Let me take you out for fish and chips. We can start in again after dinner."

At a hole-in-the-wall decorated with fishing nets, Marty, as was her habit in all social situations, regaled them with tales of her trials. Usually, it bored Meg, but tonight she was glad there was something to fill what would otherwise have been a depressed silence.

Back at Meg's, Marty paced. Jody stared into space. Meg chewed her nails. Marty taped a pencil on a yellow pad. Jody curled up in a ball. Meg chewed her lip.

"Look, . . . maybe if I sleep on it . . ." Marty flipped open her appointment book. "I don't have anything till noon tomorrow. How about if I sleep over again?"

"Great!" Mag was ready to jump at anything.

"So, I can go to sleep?" Jody stood up, almost staggering.

"Why don't you go get in my bed . . . I'm going to stay up and talk to Marty for awhile." After Jody had closed the door, Meg turned to Marty. "What are we going to do?"

"I'm just hoping she'll think of something when she's not so tired. I'll do my best . . . but I need something, Meg, someplace to begin. Right now, it's so wide open . . ." She shrugged helplessly, before her innate efficiency took over, and she stretched her long frame out on the couch. "Get some sleep, Meg. Things really do look better in the morning. I figure if I can't think, I might as well sleep."

21
To Sleep . . .
Perchance to Dream

Meg crawled in beside Jody, who had wrapped herself cocoon-style in a blanket. Exhausted, frustrated, almost feverish, she tossed restlessly before she fell asleep.

She was floating down the beach, in a surrealistic replay of the day of the accident. The groups of women streamed by, an occasional dog, a few stray men. Then the woman on the log with the glinting diamond ring—her face blew up in size and floated over Meg, the mouth grinning, the eyes fixated on her with incomprehensible hate.

Suddenly awake, Meg opened her eyes wide. There was something she had to remember. It was very important . . . so important. What was it? A name . . . She stumbled out of bed and into the living room. Marty came back to consciousness as Meg shook her, shouting "Patricia Johnston!" over and over in her face.

They were all awake again, hands clasping hot coffee mugs.

"Patricia Johnston . . . it would be incredible." Marty shook her head in amazement. "I've been following her escapades for over a year. In addition to her anti-choice activities, she's a real thorn in the side of the gay community. She goes around to liberal businesses every month and tries to carry off the lesbian and gay newspapers."

"What? That sounds pretty batty." Jody actually looked alert.

"Oh, it gets better. She's been charged with vandalizing the car of one of the volunteers for the downtown clinic."

"That's great! What do we do now? Go to the police?" Meg was almost jumping up and down with excitement.

"Meg, hold on. First, we have to wait till morning. You're sure the clinic can verify that she wasn't there the day of the gathering?" Marty looked skeptical, but Meg nodded enthusiastically. "Even if we can verify that, we have no assurances they would see this as anything other than a ploy to shift the blame, or at least cast doubt on Jody's guilt. Let's see if we can figure out some way to put this together for them so they can't ignore it." Marty sounded so reasonable.

"So, how do we begin?" asked Meg.

"First, can you verify that she was at the clinic the day you escorted?"

"Sure. I have Linda's work number. If I get her, she can call the clinic, and they can check the records for that both days. I'll call her first thing in the morning." Meg glared at the clock, that seemed to taunt her with its luminous face. It was only 3:08 a.m.

"Okay, give me the couch back. Everybody, sleep till morning." Marty stretched out again under the afghan. "I'm a pragmatist, ladies. Sleep when and if you can. I suggest you follow my example."

At 7:00 a.m., Meg was on the phone to Linda. At 9:15, she got a call back. She listened briefly, then gave the others the thumbs-up sign and hung up.

"Okay. It pans out. She was definitely there the day I escorted, and there's no record of her there the day of the gathering. Now what?"

Marty continued where she had left off in the middle of the night. "It seems to me that if she's vandalized cars before, she could be the one who vandalized Jody's van. She could easily have identified it as an 'enemy' vehicle because of the bumper stickers."

Jody jumped in. "That fits. Meg and I both have One in ten on our bumpers. Anyone who is as homophobic as this lady sounds would certainly know what that meant. Now what?"

"Well, . . ." Marty spoke slowly and methodically. "Even if a lab were able to take fingerprints from the van, and—since this is a murder investigation, they probably have—unless Patricia's fingerprints are on file, they wouldn't link her to them."

Meg sighed, leaning back into the couch. Suddenly, she leaned forward again. "But, Marty, they might be on my brake cable, too. Who else could have done it? And you saw me pick up the old cable today. It's still in a plastic bag in the back of the truck."

Marty was thoughtful. "That's right. I could corroborate your taking the truck in and picking it up and having to tow it out of the ditch. We could get the gas station attendant to testify and identify the cable. There's probably a tag on the cable. And so far, you've had no opportunity to take out the cable and replace it with another one since you got it. We've been together the whole time." She grinned and patted her back pocket. "And I've been sleeping on my keys, so I know you didn't take my car and go back over to the jail in the middle of the night."

Meg shivered. "This sounds like a spy thriller."

Marty's eyebrows shot up. "It's real life, Meg. Did you lock the truck when we got out at the police station?"

"Yes, I always do."

"Good. That means that, if it's still locked, no one else has had access either. The next step is to have someone with impeccable credentials and a good reputation examine your cable to see if they can lift any prints. I have a friend, Kelly Browning, who works for the state forensics lab in Salem. I used her last year in an abuse case. Let me give her a call right now."

Marty took the phone and disappeared into the kitchen, coming back several minutes later with a huge grin on her face. "We're in luck. Kelly was in and told me to bring the cable right over. Give me your keys, Meg. I'll go by the police station and get the brake cable, then take it over personally. Kelly said she would have the results by ten tonight." She looked at her watch. "I've gotta run if I'm going to be in Portland by noon."

"Hey, wait a minute, Marty. I don't want to get stuck here without my truck. Take me with you, and I can drive it back. Jody, I'll be back within an hour. Or do you want to come along for the ride?"

Jody shuddered. "No, thanks. I don't think I'm ready to see that place again for a long time. I'll be fine here. I could use a walk on the beach. The tide's out."

When Meg returned, Jody was lying on the couch, half asleep. She started when the door opened.

"It's just me, Jody." Meg walked into the living room. "Mind if I grab a corner of the couch?"

"No." Jody moved her feet, and Meg sat down. Jody, fatigue lines etched around her eyes, spoke in almost a whisper. "Do you really think we stand a chance, Meg?"

"Absolutely. I met Patricia, and I know she would have done it if she'd had the opportunity. She's a crazy, hate-filled woman. Let's just keep our fingers crossed that we can find some air-tight way to prove it."

"Look, Meg, I'm not sure I can just sit around all day waiting. Is it okay if I try to get some sleep? I feel like I'm never going to catch up."

Meg looked at her closely, at the worry lines, the droop of her shoulders, the flat voice. "Sounds like a good idea, Jody. Why don't you go on into the bedroom and climb under the covers? I think I'll just sit out here and try to pass the time somehow."

"Thanks, Meg. Let me know when Marty knows—no matter what the news is."

"Of course. Now get out of here and get some sleep."

22
What's in a Name?

The day dragged, a burden of endless time Meg swam through helplessly, trying not to drown. She started to read but threw the book down when she realized she'd gotten to the middle with no idea what the plot was. She started to clean out the refrigerator but wandered away with the jars and bottles lined up on the counter. Ordinarily, she might walk the beach, letting the sea soothe her as only it could, but today she was attached to the phone as if it were her umbilical cord. The call might come early—there was no telling.

From time to time, she looked in on Jody, who had somehow managed to fall into a deep sleep. She roused herself briefly around dinnertime to gulp down a glass of milk before going comatose again. Jail, thought Meg, must have been the ultimate humiliation.

Sunset came, and Marty had still not phoned. The clock ticked away the hours: 9:00 p.m., 9:30, 10:15, 11:00, 11:08. Ring! Meg, poised all day for this one sound, an animal focused on nothing but her prey, lifted the receiver. But it wasn't Marty. It was Kim, her voice quavering as it had so often. Suddenly for Meg, no time had passed at all. "Don't hang up, Meg, please."

"What is it?" Meg's voice was flat, her mind numb.

"It's about Susan and this . . . accident."

"Susan? What has that got to do with you?" All the anger never expressed welled up in Meg.

"Meg, please, just listen. I need your help."

How many times had she heard that before? She would have slammed the phone down, but anything about Susan she needed to hear about. "Okay. I'm listening."

"Meg, did you know Cheryl and Susan were in the same alcohol treatment program?" Meg didn't answer, listening silently and stoically. Kim continued. "Well, they were, and I went to the group where everyone brought their partners,"—

Meg winced—"and I met Susan. And then, there were a few parties. To make a long story short, Susan came on to me." Meg drew in her breath. "*I* didn't do anything, but Cheryl got so angry. Meg, she's worse sober than she was drunk."

"What's the point here?" Meg's voice was harsh, but her heart felt ripped from her chest. "Then why didn't you choose me, you fool!" she wanted to scream.

"Well, remember the get-together on the beach? When we drove up, Cheryl saw your truck, and then she saw Susan's. Susan had dropped out of treatment when she started drinking, so Cheryl never got to confront her with her feelings."

Well, this was certainly a new language for the world's most indirect person. Suddenly, something in what Kim had said hit Meg. "Kim, why should my truck bother her? She didn't know we were lovers."

Kim swallowed hard. "Yeah, she did. Somebody told her—she never told me who—and she confronted me in group, and . . . well, she knew."

Meg sat digesting this new piece of information, as well as the strange sound of the word 'confront' coming from Kim's mouth twice in just a few sentences. Kim went on.

"She was so angry, Meg. She was livid, she was . . ." Kim apparently couldn't find a word intense enough, and her voice trailed off for a minute. "She said she was going for a walk. She was gone for a couple of hours, and when she came back, she seemed . . . calm. Real calm. Cheryl doesn't just calm down like that. So, when I heard about the cut wires in Susan's van, I thought . . . well, . . . you know Cheryl always has tools in the truck. But since you were okay, I thought it probably wasn't her, because she was even more furious at you than she was at Susan." There was a hopeful upswing in Kim's voice; clearly, she wanted Meg to somehow make it okay, as she had so often in the past. But the past was gone.

Meg gripped the phone with white-knuckled hands. "She did, Kim. She did cut the wires on my truck."

"Oh my God, . . ." Kim was sobbing now.

Meg had to force herself to keep breathing. "Is that why you called, to find out if I was still alive, or if your maniac lover had killed me, too?"

"No . . . yes . . . I mean . . . the thing is . . ." Kim was speaking between bursts of tears. "Cheryl says she spent that time with an old friend named Lisa who had moved to the coast. Right after she saw the two trucks, she took off down the beach. It was still afternoon. I waited awhile in the parking lot. Then, I went for a long walk on the beach. We didn't meet up again until after dark near the bonfire. If she really was with this person, she couldn't have done it, right?" Again, hope glinted through Kim's tears.

"I don't know any Lisa. I'll check . . . but, Kim, it all fits. It makes this whole crazy thing make sense. I didn't even know Susan. How else would Susan and I be connected? This is . . . Kim, I can't really grasp this yet. I have to go, I have to get off the phone."

"Will you check . . . about this Lisa?" Kim was timid.

"I said I would. I really have to go."

She was putting the receiver down as she heard Kim's voice. "I miss you, Meg."

Meg went into the bedroom and stroked Jody's arm until she groggily opened her eyes. "I'm sorry, Jody, I have to ask you something; it's important." Jody nodded sleepily. "How long have you lived on the coast?"

"Six or seven years."

"Do you know any lesbian who lives around here named Lisa?"

Jody sucked her cheeks in thoughtfully. "Unh-unh."

"If there had been someone at the gathering named Lisa, would you have known for sure?"

"There aren't many of us here, Meg. I don't see how . . . I knew everybody there who was from the coast. What's up?"

"Not much. Go back to sleep. No big deal."

Jody didn't need much of an invitation. She was asleep again before Meg had the door closed.

Meg stood in the middle of the living room. She had to deal with this inside herself before she could tell Jody. She was in shock, she knew. She went to the kitchen sink and threw cold water on herself, drenching her sweatshirt in the process. Shivering, she pulled off the shirt and wrapped herself in the afghan draped over the back of the couch, turned off the light, and sat in the darkened living room. "Cheryl tried to kill me. Cheryl did kill Susan." There, she had said it out loud.

A strange feeling of exaltation was creeping over her. Cheryl, who had taken Kim . . . now, Cheryl would be taken from Kim. They would both suffer, wouldn't they? And Kim—Kim hated to be alone. If Cheryl went to prison, Kim would come crawling back . . . and Meg would laugh in her face. Patricia Johnston—God, had they been on the wrong track. Marty hadn't even bothered to call back. What a bunch of idiot amateurs. Exhausted beyond words, she stretched out on the couch and slept.

She was standing up to her knees in the ocean. From somewhere out to sea, she heard Kim's voice cry for help. Or was it Jody's? "I'm coming," she called, struggling through the waves. As the water reached her chest, something rose from the sea, looming over her. "Cheryl, no . . ." She lost her footing, her head went under . . . under . . .

Meg woke with a start. The living room was pitch black. Had she heard a noise? There it was again, by the corner of the house. She held her breath, suspended. Nothing now, nothing . . . maybe it was her imagination. Her nerves were certainly shot. She began to breath again, and then something knocked against the porch steps. Her heart beat wildly. She could see the steps vividly in her imagination, the pop can she had left sitting on the side of the top step, just where someone would kick it over trying to avoid the squeaking planks in the middle.

Suddenly, she knew clearly who it was. Cheryl had overheard the phone call. God only knew what she had done to Kim, and now she was here to make sure the only other person who knew never told. Meg looked at the luminous dial of her watch. An hour to take care of Kim—what has she done to you, Kim?—and another two to get here. The timing was right.

Breathlessly, she crept to the kitchen and slipped her hand into a drawer, grasping her sharpest knife. Hugging the wall, she stepped back into the living room, around the front window. Biting her lower lip to stop her shaking, she lifted the edge of the curtain and flipped on the porch light at the same time. The porch seemed empty until she looked down. There was the fattest raccoon she had ever seen lapping up the remains of her pop.

She let the shaking take her over now, laughing and crying, muffling her mouth with the curtain so as not to wake Jody. She threw the knife onto the coffee table and wrapped herself

110

in the afghan again. She might as well get comfortable; there would be no more sleep for her tonight, she knew.

Dawn found her exhausted and defeated. The absurd sense of gloating from the night before had vanished, leaving in its place the ashes of bitterness. Was this what it meant to be a lesbian then—not only betrayal, but now murder? She felt sick of herself, of Jody, of Kim, of all of it. Today, she had to dress, go to the police station, turn someone in. Turn in a lesbian. Let them take the brake cable and get the damned fingerprints; she was tired of playing Nancy Drew.

In the cold light of dawn, Kim's story about Cheryl's rendezvous with a woman named Lisa seemed phantasmagoric. Meg would let the police take it from here. Having another lesbian to investigate would make their day.

Dressing quietly, she left Jody a note and slipped out to the truck. In Newbridge, she circled the police station, then drove down to the public beach and parked. Maybe a walk would help her get up her nerve.

It was a quiet, sunny morning, the beach almost deserted. She took great strides and deep breaths, trying to cleanse herself. It took her a minute to recognize the voice calling her name.

"Meg! Hey!" She turned and watched Crystal alternately running and walking down the beach. "You looked like you were getting ready for a race!" Crystal laughed, breathless.

"Ummm . . ." Meg started out toward the ocean, not wanting the intrusion, but Crystal was oblivious to being snubbed.

"I walk every morning, and then I go over to Starbuck's and have a hot, thick cup of black coffee." She rolled her eyes. "My greatest vice." She linked her arm in Meg's. "Wanna come?"

Meg sighed. Why not? She had actually forgotten coffee this morning, a first for her.

They cleared the morning paper from a table by the window and sat over their steaming cups, inhaling, a coffee lover's ritual. Well, Meg thought, I guess I should give this 'Lisa' business one last try. I'm not really excited about talking to the police. "Crystal, . . ." Meg didn't look up. "Do you know a lesbian at the coast named Lisa?"

Crystal took her first sip and shuddered with pleasure. "No, and I do know everyone."

Meg looked out the window. The day was clear, but she felt shrouded in fog. She glanced wearily back at Crystal and caught a self-contained smile on her lips. Was she feeling smug about being such a community fixture, someone who knew everyone? Another time, Meg might have found it amusing. Now, she took a sip of her coffee, wishing it were scalding enough to distract her with pain. Cheryl was guilty; Jody would go free. Why didn't it make her as happy now as it had last night?

"It's funny," Crystal was saying, "your bringing up the name Lisa."

"Funny? How?" Meg tried to swim back through the fog, forcing herself to talk.

"I don't usually tell people . . . I mean, it's not who I am anymore, you know? But before I changed it to Crystal, my name was Lisa."

Meg sat bolt upright, the fog clearing in an instant. "Crystal, do you know Cheryl Forbes?"

"Oh, yeah. We go way back. She never would call me Crystal—still calls me Lisa." She stood up. "I need a refill."

Meg had to keep herself from hauling Crystal back into her chair. Finally, full cup in hand, Crystal seated herself again.

Meg tried to act nonchalant. "The infamous gathering . . . did you get to talk to Cheryl there?"

Crystal nodded. "We had a long walk before the bonfire. She needed to talk. Her lover," here she shook her head, "Whew!, had one affair and then another one after she was in treatment. At least, Cheryl thought she did. Kim . . . she's bad news." She shook her head again. "Cheryl's so patient with her. I think she's crazy to stay with her, but she's real hung up on her, I guess."

Cheryl, the Cheryl she had heard so much about, patient? And Kim, bad news? How she had simplified things. She doubted that either she or Crystal had a clear picture, but it was becoming evident that the story was more complex than she had realized. "Crystal, how long were you two together that day?"

Crystal didn't seem to wonder why she was being given the third degree. "A couple of hours, I guess. We walked down the beach all the way to Sheldon Park."

Sheldon Park. It was three or four miles from the parking lot, Meg guessed. "You said she was upset, Crystal. Did she calm down?"

"Oh, yeah. I'm a pretty good listener. She was a lot better by the time we got back. We separated a little before you and Jody came back. I saw Kim in the distance and took off as fast as I could. She just isn't one of my favorite people. A few minutes later, they came to the campfire together. I guess they had patched things up again." Crystal shrugged. "I sure don't understand it. I guess I'm not very enlightened about Kim, am I?" She laughed. Meg smiled, really smiled, for the first time that morning. Crystal really did twitter, she thought, but she liked it.

Outside and alone, Meg walked along a downtown street. Cheryl hadn't killed anybody, or even tried to, and, God, she was glad! They'd get Jody off, but not this way. Her faith in lesbians restored, Meg whistled as she went into a shop and bought a postcard with a pelican sitting on a wharf on it. Down the street, she went into the post office and leaned against the counter as she filled it out. "Found Lisa. Alibi good." She paused. Then she added, "Take care of yourself."

She bought a stamped envelope, addressed it with the address she knew by heart, and put the postcard in. She stood for a minute, holding the envelope. "Goodbye, Kim," she said under her breath. "Goodbye, goodbye, goodbye." Then she slid the envelope into the slot and walked out into the sun. She had to get home and call Marty; the three lesbian musketeers had work to do.

23
Fair's Fair

It was mid-morning when Meg opened the front door of the cabin, a quart of milk under her arm. Noises, cooking noises, emanated from the kitchen, along with the smell of fresh coffee. It was the nicest homecoming she'd had in a long time.

Jody, with one of Meg's T-shirts hanging to mid-thigh and flour smeared across her cheek, looked up sheepishly as Meg paused in the kitchen doorway. "Bread," she grinned, slapping the fat roll of dough on the counter before her. "Very well-kneaded bread." Meg grinned back, the joy of finding this beautiful woman so at home in her kitchen almost more than she could bear. "And now that you're back," Jody gave the bread a final slap, "I'll start breakfast." She scowled at Meg. "You didn't go out for breakfast, did you?"

Meg just shook her head, struck almost speechless by the change in Jody. Marty was right; it was amazing what a good night's sleep could do. Any thought she might have had of telling Jody about her wild goose chase fled; it seemed like nothing but a strange dream as she watched the sunlight streaming through the window dance across Jody's blond hair.

Half an hour later, they were eating bacon, cheese omelettes, and toast dripping with butter. "You've been taking care of me," Jody said between bites. "I don't usually let anybody do that. I'm one of those hermit crabs, you know—picked up this shell and walked around with it. But I guess I've never been down this low. I don't know how to thank you, Meg."

Meg took time to chew her bacon. "I guess I'm one of those crabs myself. I mean, it's not easy for me to reach out." She looked down, examining her plate intently. "But with you it's been easy."

Jody put down her fork, rested her elbows on the table and propped her chin in her hands. "I felt so at ease that day we met . . . like . . . I don't know . . . like we knew some language nobody else did." She sighed. "I felt so free with you . . . like I didn't have to think about what I said or monitor myself. That's how I usually feel around people. I felt like I could have walked that beach forever, showing you every special, secret place I know." She stopped abruptly and picked up her fork again, focused on her omelette.

But Meg just continued to stare, warmth spreading across her chest. "You did show me a special, secret place," she said softly. "You showed me you." Jody looked up again, and their eyes met and held. When Meg finally realized the phone was ringing, her eyes opened wider in a sudden remembrance. "Marty!" She jumped up and grabbed the receiver.

"So, where were you, out on a fishing boat?" Marty grumbled. "This phone rang fifteen times!"

"Give it up, Marty. You're only a day late yourself."

"Hey, I tried. You were on the phone for God knows how long last night. A dyke's gotta get her beauty sleep. I was in court this morning; just got out, or I'd have called sooner. Anyway, it's good news. Kelly lifted three sets of prints."

"Great! Now what?"

"Well, I expect yours might be one of them, if you examined it."

"Yes, I did, when I was fooling around with it to see if the cable was loose."

"Then the next one would be the gas station attendant's, and we could probably get his permission to get his fingerprints. If not, we can use legal means.

"Then," Marty paused, we just have one set to go. Let's hope they're Patricia Johnston's. They would have no logical explanation for being under your hood."

"Sounds wonderful. When are you coming back out here?"

"I'll be there tomorrow morning. Get a good night's sleep, and then we can figure out how to get a usable set of Patricia's prints."

"Whooppee!" Meg shouted as she hung up the phone. She looked toward Jody a moment and then dialed again. "Mrs. Green, it's Meg. I've had kind of an emergency come up. I wonder if Sally could switch some shifts with me." Sally, fortunately, was at that moment sweeping in front of the office. In a few minutes, the arrangements were made, and Meg had a few weeks freedom in exchange for taking over Sally's shifts the following two weeks. Sally wanted the time off to visit her sister.

Meg hung up and turned back to Jody triumphantly. "For the next two weeks, I'm your full-time private detective!"

They spent the afternoon lazing on the porch, as comfortable as they had been that first day. By unspoken agreement, the avoided talking about the case, reminiscing instead about childhoods, schools, families and lovers. As dusk approached, Meg went out and brought back a pizza. "There *is* other food in the world," Jody teased her. They ate slowly, watching the sun set. "You look tired." Jody peered intently through the growing gloom at Meg, who just nodded. Last night's escapade was catching up with her.

Grabbing her by the arm, Jody led her back into the bedroom. Too tired to protest, Meg lay down on the covers. "Join me, Jody. This bed is wide enough for two, as we've already proven."

"Sure, move over . . . but take those scratchy pants off."

"Yes, ma'am. Glad to oblige." Meg looked up at Jody. "That goes for you, too."

"Guess you're right. Fair's fair." She giggled. "We'll both take your pants off." She slipped easily out of the baggy sweats she had borrowed, while Meg struggled out of her jeans. Within moments, Jody and Meg were holding each other, content to rest in each other's arms. Sleep came swiftly and gently, before either had a chance to savor or wonder about their being together again in a bed that was made for more things than sleep.

24
Baiting the Trap

The next thing Meg heard was someone pounding on the front door. Groggily, she opened her eyes to peer under the blinds. "It's Marty."

Jody rolled over to face Meg. "Here we go again, partner. Ready for the day?"

"You better believe it! Let's get up and moving."

Meg's pants had slid to the far corner of the bed; Jody's were crumpled on the floor. Within a few seconds, they were both stumbling toward the door, pulling themselves together as they went. Meg opened the door. Marty stood there, arms full.

"I thought we could get right to work if I brought breakfast." She thrust two bulging bags into Meg and Jody's arms. "Here's a quart of milk, fresh orange juice, and an assortment of goodies I got at Colonial Bakery. Let's see . . ." They had moved in concert to the living room. "I got poppyseed muffins, bear claws, buttermilk bars and chocolate donuts. Something for everyone."

Meg's eyes sparkled. "How did you know I'm addicted to their poppyseed cakes? They must use opium poppies."

After placing the donuts on napkins, Marty gave them a closer look. "My, my, you two certainly look cozy."

Meg blushed. "We *did* manage to get a good night's sleep."

"Not on the couch, I bet."

Meg took a deep breath and glared at Marty. "Would you like your coffee in your cup or over your head."

Jody just smiled. "I'm so glad to know I have such a perceptive lawyer."

Marty raised her infamous eyebrow and switched topics. "All right." She was all business now. "Let's figure out where we go from here. We'll start with what we know and prove the rest. We have three sets of prints to identify. Kelly gave me a fingerprint kit for me to take yours, Meg, and an extra for the gas station attendant. Assuming they match, that leaves us with one unknown person, hopefully Patricia. If they match, we'll go one from there."

"So, what do we do to get them? Walk up to her and say, 'Hi, I'm accused of murdering my lover, but we think you did it. Can we have a copy of your fingerprints?'" Jody's voice was sarcastic.

Marty laughed. "Sure, if you think it would work. Seriously though, I do have an idea, if you're willing, Meg."

"Me? What can I do?"

"You've already met her, and you encounter her every weekend you're a clinic escort. When's your next shift?"

"Ah," Meg paused. "I think it isn't for three or four more weeks."

"Well, we can't wait that long. Can you switch with somebody and go in this weekend?"

"I don't see why not. Why, what's your plan?"

"How good are you at acting?"

Meg was suddenly suspicious. "Why?"

"I got an idea last night while I was waiting to get back Kelly's report. I have a friend who's a free-lance photographer and does videos of things like weddings. I plan to station her in a car across the street from the clinic. She can record everything. I'll be there with her, along with a couple of other reliable witnesses, including a notary public."

"Why a notary public?" Jody and Meg questioned in unison.

"I'll explain in a minute. I want you on duty as usual, wearing a light sweater. You'll have with you an unopened package containing a plastic windbreaker," Marty continued. "When it's time for your shift to end, come outside and signal us. We'll make sure you're being taped. Take the jacket out of the package and put it on. It doesn't matter if you get your own prints on it, just get as few on it as possible. We can take your prints later to match them. Then, when you walk to the corner to get into your truck, let Patricia bait you into a response. Get into a shouting match with her. Use your imagination."

Meg laughed. "I've wanted to call her lots of names ever since I met her. That won't be any trouble."

"Listen carefully, Meg. There's more. You mustn't shove her. We can't risk jeopardizing the clinic's lawsuit, but I don't think it's going to take much to push her over the edge. You have to get her to touch you." Meg shuddered.

Marty went on. "As soon as she shoves you—make sure you can feel her hands against your jacket—break away and come over to the car. I'll step outside while my friend is taping, then you take off the jacket, fold it inside out and place it in a container I'll give you. Seal it, then the notary public will put it inside a large manila envelope, place a wax seal over the slit and sign it. Then, my attorney friend and I will drive straight to Salem, where Kelly will be waiting for us."

"That sounds great!" Jody was excited. She turned to Meg. "Are you up to it, Meg? This woman sounds pretty crazy."

"There's only one way to find out. I'll give the volunteer coordinator a call right now to switch my shift." Meg came back in a couple of minutes, a swagger in her walk. "It's all arranged. I'm on for nine o'clock this Saturday."

"Okay." Marty relaxed. "Meet me at Dugan's at eight, and we can go over it one more time."

"It's a date. See you then. Is there anything else we have to do before then?"

"No, Meg. Just keep hanging in there and relax as much as you can." Marty stood up, brushing crumbs off her shirt. "Well, I have to get back to Portland. I had to postpone some meetings with clients to spring free the last couple of days."

Jody stood up too, holding out her hand. "Thanks for coming, Marty. I don't know what we would have done without you."

"My pleasure. See you soon."

After Marty's truck pulled away, Meg turned back to Jody. "Stay with me here, Jody, at least until we know what happens this weekend. I don't want the whole town gawking at you, and," she added, eyes softening, "I want you to be here with me. I've grown accustomed to your face."

"Meg, . . . we have to talk." Jody walked over to the window, took a few deep breaths and swallowed hard. "This is hard to talk about . . . but I have to." She grabbed the curtain tight in her fists before going on. "When Susan died, I'd had it. That's what we were talking about in the van that night.

I'd tried, but I was finished. Our walk that day . . . you and me . . ." Tears were runnings down her cheeks. "I realized what it could feel like to feel good with somebody, to feel happy." She bit her lip, turning to Meg. "You were . . . you know . . . just like the period at the end of a sentence. I already knew the sentence, what I had to say. Being with you just made it so . . . final. And then she died." Jody was sobbing. "God damn it, right after I told her I wanted to break up, she died! Do you have any idea how guilty I feel? No, don't touch me right now . . ." She was quivering, but she pushed Meg's outstretched arms away. "I need to work this through inside myself, Meg. It's so unfinished. I'm not free, do you understand? You've been great . . . wonderful . . . I can hardly believe somebody cares this much. But I'm not free."

"Look, Jody, you're going through so much . . ." Meg fumbled, wanting nothing right now but to hold Jody and take away a pain she had no control over. "Can we just take it day by day? I'm here for you now. So is this place. We don't have to think past the next two weeks."

"Really?" Jody took a deep gulp of air. "Are you sure?"

"Really." Meg gave her a little punch on the arm. "Now start earning your keep and help me clean up this mess."

Jody, her sobbing diminished to sniffles, looked around. "We have managed to trash it, haven't we? Okay, captain, hand me a broom."

"A broom, hell, we need a shovel." Through tears, rent hearts, confusion and uncertainty, they actually grinned at each other.

25
Springing the Trap

A week of time out of time, time suspended, a cocoon spun almost unknowingly to cradle Jody and Meg as they grew and changed imperceptibly into something different from what either could imagine or become alone. They slept as late as they wanted, cooked leisurely meals, listened to music, walked on the beach after dark when they were safe from prying eyes. Together, they worked on the cabins. Jody was teaching Meg basic wiring, something she'd been terrified of ever since she'd tried to fix a lamp years before and forgotten to unplug it.

When they were working side by side, Meg sensed a Jody more sure of herself struggling to the surface. Yet, whenever Lloyd, the cabin owner, showed up or a confused tourist used the driveway to turn around or tried to ask directions, Jody would slip unobtrusively away, leaving Meg to deal with the intruder.

The last night had been fitful for Meg, fearful images of the upcoming day invading her restless sleep. Even before the alarm sounded, she was up and moving. Next to her, Jody rolled over, barely stirring, her deep slumber a sign of trust.

Two cups of coffee later, with a fresh cup on the counter ready for the trip, Meg tiptoed to the door of the bedroom, hesitated, then moved softly over to the bed. Kneeling next to the still sleeping form, she gently stroked Jody's cheek.

"Jody," she whispered softly, "Jody . . ."

Jody, rolling over, opened her eyes and held open her arms. "Is it time to go already?"

Kneeling by the bed, Meg lowered her head to Jody's breasts. "Yes, it's almost six."

Jody wrapped her arms tightly around Meg. "Nervous?"

Meg laughed weakly. "Of course. I'm not crazy, just foolhardy."

"Are you sure you don't want me to go with you?"

"Absolutely. I agree with Marty that you need to be far away. I'll call you as soon as I can. I should be home by early afternoon."

Meg started to rise, but Jody wouldn't let go. "Here's one for the road then." Jody, holding Meg's head in her hands, pulled her close and kissed her on the lips.

Meg was startled. The kiss was tender yet insistent, and Meg had only a moment to respond before their lips parted. Although they had cuddled a lot, slept in the same bed and held hands a few times in the past week, Jody had seemed hesitant to go any further, and Meg knew better than to push her.

"Well," Meg finally said in what she hoped sounded like a businesslike tone, "I really need to get going. I have to be in town by eight. Take care of yourself. I'll call as soon as I know anything." Reluctantly, she rose. Winking at Jody, she shut the bedroom door, grabbed her coffee and breakfast bar and went out to the truck.

All the way to Portland, Meg elaborated on the fantasies inspired by Jody's unexpected kiss. At 7:45, Meg pulled up outside Dugan's, without remembering exactly how she had gotten there.

The place held a lot of memories for her. She had eaten her first meal with Kim there, and Kim had grasped her hand there for the first time when she told Meg she was falling in love with her. Today, however, the ghosts were gone, the memories held no sting; now they were just a part of her former life. Spotting Marty, Meg waved aside the waiter, joining Marty next to the window.

"You made good time. How's Jody doing?"

Meg paused. "It was a strange week. She's been struggling with herself. Sometimes, she seems like her old self; at other times, she seems paralyzed, like a sleepwalker."

"That's understandable. How is she supposed to live her life with the suspicion of her lover's death hanging over her like a black cloud?"

Meg sighed. "Yeah, I guess you're right. We'll both be relieved when today is over. I really want to do it, but I'm getting nervous. I'm afraid I'm going to screw up."

Marty reasured her. "You're going to be fine. There is no danger, and with a little bit of luck we'll be able to nail Patricia. Now order some breakfast so we can get going."

The waiter hovered next to her, menu in hand, but Meg already knew what she wanted. "Home fries with cheese, please, and coffee with cream." That had been her old standby when she and Kim had eaten here. As the waiter returned with her cream, Meg smiled as she had the first time she had seen the container, a baby bottle with the nipple cut down.

As they ate, Marty tackling the house omelette, they went over the procedure one last time, until they were both sure Meg knew it thoroughly. Glancing at her watch, Marty shoved her plate away. "Time to go." The large grandfather clock chimed the half-hour: 8:30. Standing up, Marty looked at Meg. "Ready?"

Meg, taking one last swig of coffee, pushed herself away from the table. "Yes. Let's go."

Traffic was still light. It took only a few minutes for them to cross town. As they circled the block, Meg, scrunched down a bit in the passenger's seat, saw several picketers already in place, waving their signs at passing motorists. It was easy to spot Patricia. She was already on the corner, thrusting her *Honk if you hate abortion* sign into the traffic.

"Did you spot your friends?" Meg asked.

"Yes, they're right across the street from the front door. I'm going to park a couple of blocks away. Then you can circle around the other way to get to the clinic, while I approach them from the other side."

After locking up, Marty turned to Meg. "Good luck. We'll see you in a couple of hours. Here's the windbreaker."

"Thanks." As Marty walked briskly away, a wave of panic washed over Meg. Knees rubbery, she abandoned the security of Marty's truck for an alleyway lined with sagging chainlink fences and overflowing garbage bags. As the opening to the street loomed ahead, Meg paused. Time to give herself a pep talk. "Look," she mumbled under her breath, "I know you're scared. That's perfectly natural. But you're going to be fine. You're not in danger, and if you do it right, Jody may end up having murder charges dropped."

Straightening her shoulders and finding a spring in her step, she strode out onto the sidewalk and turned toward the clinic. Her determination and speed caught the protestors off guard, and she was in the door before they had a chance to shout at her.

The lounge was deserted. Finding a spare vest, Meg put it on and went back outside. Today, she would work only inside the injunction area. There would be enough action later. Soon she fell into the rhythm of spotting women who seemed like potential clients, sidling nonchalantly to their side and easing them toward the door. Railing protestors tried to provoke her, but Meg was elsewhere, deep inside, centering herself for what lay ahead.

Before she knew it, the second shift had arrived, going inside to get reports from the volunteer coordinator. Left alone on the sidewalk except for the picketers, Meg looked across the street to see Marty giving the thumbs-up signal. Meg nodded and went inside as soon as the new volunteers emerged. Usually, she took a few moments to visit with them, but not today. She took off her vest, picking up her still unopened package and stepped outside. Making sure she could see the camera focused on her, Meg ripped open the sealed package, trying to touch only the collar. Fortunately, it wasn't zipped, so she shook it out a bit and put her arms inside the sleeves. Gingerly, Meg pulled up the zipper, making sure she didn't touch the outside of the jacket. For once, she was grateful for the Oregon weather, a slight, moist breeze making it seem natural to put on extra clothing.

Well, it was now or never! No volunteers were yet in place on the corner. She had better move fast because she didn't want to involve them or the clinic. Walking toward the corner, Meg saw the woman with the camera get out of the van and follow her from across the street. Fortunately, the picketers were focused on the clinic door and seemed unaware of her.

It took just a moment to catch Patricia's eye. She was still on the corner, isolated from the other picketers. Spotting Meg, she turned to face her. "Murderer! Baby-killer!" She waved her poster of a mutilated fetus under Meg's nose.

Meg looked her straight in the eye. "You're crazy. Do you know that?" Not brilliant by any means, but effective. Patricia looked as if she had been slapped.

"Dyke! Lesbian! Lezzie butch! You're going to burn in hell!"

"If *you're* going to heaven, I'd *rather* be in hell. You make me sick."

Patricia kept coming closer, her flushed face tightening in rage. "God's judgment is coming, and there is no escape for the wicked."

It wouldn't take much more to push her over the edge. Meg reached under the collar, careful not to smudge her windbreaker, and pulled out her goddess medallion. "You can take your Father God and shove it. Here's a picture of my Goddess." That did it. The poster fell from Patricia's hand, and she came at Meg, pushing hard at her chest with her open hands. "Pagan witch! Baby-killer!"

Meg kept taunting her, pushing back with her body against Patricia's increasingly harder shoves. "I'm not going to roll over and play dead for you, Christian bitch!"

Patricia was livid. She grabbed Meg's arm with both hands, but Meg managed to twist away, turning her back on Patricia. She wasn't fast enough. Patricia shoved her one last time between the shoulder blades, almost knocking Meg to the ground.

Meg turned back one last time. As Patricia went for her eyes, Meg got her forearm up. "You're evil! You're not even human! Whore! Bitch! Fornicator!" Patricia shouted.

It was time to leave. This time, Meg turned and sprinted between two parked cars, calling out over her shoulder, "You're the evil one!"

When she got to the van, the side door was open and the engine was running. A voice came from within. "Get in!" They pulled away just as Patricia came running towards the driver's side, screams still spewing forth from her mouth. They pulled away quickly, flinging Meg to the floor.

A few blocks away, they pulled over. As soon as they came to a complete stop, Marty gave Meg instructions. "Okay, Meg, take off your jacket as carefully as you can and fold it up inside out . . . Good, now put it in this plastic bag."

As soon as Meg had done that, Marty handed the bag to a woman sitting in the back seat. She took it, sealed it with tape, put it in a large manila envelope, and sealed it. Then she took out a notary seal from her purse, stamped it and signed her name.

As soon as she had finished, Marty introduced everyone. "Meg, this is Sarah. The photographer is Jenny, and Michael is a lawyer friend."

Meg suddenly felt shy. "Hi. Uh, I really appreciate all the help you've given today. What happens now?"

Marty spoke. "Jenny will drop you, Michael and me off at my truck. I'll take you back to Dugan's, then Michael and I are going to drive straight to Salem. Kelly will be waiting for us at the lab. We should have the results by early evening."

"Sounds great! I'm tired of waiting." Meg sighed. "If this doesn't work, I don't know what to do next."

Marty turned to her. "Don't worry about that right now. Let's see what happens here first."

26
The Net Tightens

Meg raced home. As soon as she pulled in, an anxious Jody was at the door to greet her. "Well?"

Meg made the thumbs-up sign. "We did it! Everything went according to plan, and I'm sure I got some usable prints. We should know in a few hours."

"I hope it's almost over, Meg. I don't think I can stand the suspense much longer. I want my life back."

Meg put her hand on Jody's arm. "I can't much stand the waiting myself, but I'm still high from my encounter with Patricia. And I'm hungry. Is there anything for lunch?"

Jody smiled. "Follow me, Amazon woman. I have a surprise." She turned and led Meg into the living room, where the coffee table was laid out for lunch, complete with a yellow wild rose in a clear bud vase. There were cheese, bacon, lettuce, tomato, sourdough and whole wheat bread, a bowl of potato chips and soup bowls. Tears sprang to Meg's eyes. It must have been even harder for Jody to wait than for Meg to do what she had done that morning. "It's beautiful, Jody. Just what I needed."

"Well, then, my hero . . . or is it heroine? She made a mock bow. "Sit down. I'll get your soup and Dr. Pepper, and you can tell me of your amazing exploits—in great detail." Meg was ravenous. It seemed another lifetime since she had eaten. Two sandwiches later, a third partailly eaten on her plate, she leaned back.

"That was just what I needed. Are you ready to hear the details of my fight for justice?"

Jody laughed. "Are you kidding? It was all I could do to let you finish your sandwiches."

Meg settled back, drink in hand, to recount the adventures of the day. She had just gotten up to the part where the van was pulling away from the curb with Patricia chasing them when the phone rang. They both jumped, Meg knocking over her glass. She grabbed the phone in the middle of its first ring. "Hello!"

"It's Marty."

"Do you know anything yet?"

"We got a positive make on the prints. They match Patricia Johnston's. It looks like we have a case!"

"All right!" Meg turned to Jody. "They match! Now what, Marty?"

"I'm calling a press conference this evening in front of the D.A.'s office. I've notified the major papers in Salem and Portland, and they're going to have reporters there. I've also called KARG News, and they promised to send a crew. I know it's unusual to do it this way, but I don't want this evidence to not be treated seriously or to get 'lost.'"

"I don't know how he can ignore that kind of pressure, Marty. It sounds like a great idea. When do you think the charges against Jody are going to be dropped?"

"Probably not until they bring Patricia in for questioning and find out more about her movements on the day of Susan's death."

"That could take days."

"Yes, it could, but it sure beats having to go to trial. So take it easy, and let's hope something pops in the next couple of days."

"Okay, Marty. Good luck with the press."

Meg hung up the phone. "This calls for a toast. I have a bottle of Dutch Almond champagne someone gave me when I moved in. How does that sound?"

Jody looked uncomfortable.

Meg was puzzled, then dismayed. "Oh, Jody, I'm sorry. I just forgot, I got so carried away. How about a bottle of sparkling cider instead?"

"Thanks, Meg. I'm just not ready to deal with alcohol yet."

"Well, I'll put the cider in the freezer to chill while I go to the store and buy some steaks. I really feel like celebrating. Why don't you start the barbecue, and we can sit out back and watch the sunset?"

"Does your trip include baking potatoes, sour cream, salad fixings and cheesecake . . . my treat?"

Meg laughed, their awkwardness gone. "Whatever you wish. Now get busy, woman, and get those coals going. I'll be back in half an hour."

Jody followed her to the front door, wallet in hand. "Will twenty do it? Oh, and how about garlic bread, too? I better give you thirty. Suddenly, I'm famished."

"Sure. Now get busy with that fire!" Meg bounded out the door, her body coursing with energy. It was all she could do to keep from shouting out loud.

The evening passed all too swiftly. The two of them sat up late into the night, sitting on the back porch, watching the stars wheel across the sky, listening to the waves washing over the rocks. Full and content in each other's company, they tumbled into bed in the little hours of the morning, falling asleep intertwined.

It was mid-morning before they woke. Meg glanced over at the bedside clock. "Ten o'clock. Stay here. I'm going to get the paper and see if there's anything in it."

Meg was back in a few moments, paper already open. She sat on the side of the bed. "Here it is, in the Metro section."

"In a press conference called last night, Marty Stern, defense attorney for Jody Miller, accused in the death of her lover, Susan Callahan, made a surprise announcement.

"Ms. Stern disclosed that independent investigation has uncovered a prime suspect in the murder, one that police have not yet questioned.

"'The person is not a member of the women's community, where the police have been confining their investigations. We have reason to believe that the person responsible for Ms. Callahan's death was someone that the police would have had no reason to interrogate. This new evidence should be sufficient to bring the one we think is responsible in for questioning.'"

"In response to a reporter's question, Ms. Stern said that she was not going to reveal the person's name. That was a job for law enforcement agencies. She had called the press conference to focus attention on the way the case was being handled and to make sure that the evidence presented to the D.A.'s office would be given full investigation.

"The D.A. was unavailable for comment. His press secretary said that he would have an official statement in the next few hours."

"Thank Goddess," Jody expelled her breath. "It's finally over." She fairly leapt out of bed to stand, arms akimbo, in front of Meg. "We did it, you and me." Meg saw again the woman she had met that first day on the beach, strength in the tilt of the chin, fire in her eyes. Her eyes . . . was that more than appreciation Meg saw? Suddenly self-conscious, aware of her overweight body, Meg fought not to cross her arms over her "Goddesses are not anorexic" T-shirt.

She had been careful not to push Jody too far. Meg slept with her every night and held her close, but she suppressed her sexual desires. It hadn't been easy. She had wanted so much more and wondered if it would ever come. Now suddenly, Jody sat down beside her and tangled her hand in Meg's hair. With the other, she stroked her face. Her eyes were blue, blue as the sea, blue as the sky, blue enough to drown in.

Jody kissed her softly, her lips slightly parted. Meg's breath caught in her throat, her hands slid up Jody's sinewy arms. "You're beautiful," she whispered. Now Jody's mouth found the tender spot on Meg's neck, just behind the earlobe. She nibbled gently, then insistently. Meg's breath came faster. She felt Jody's hand slipping up under her T-shirt, cupping her breast, the thumb and fingers moving slowly, inexorably together, closing in on their goal, her erect, tingling nipple . . .

The phone rang. Meg jumped. Jody mumbled, her head still buried in Meg's neck, "Let it ring!" Meg tried to relax again, but the phone kept ringing. Eleven, twelve, thirteen.

"Hon, . . ." Meg's breath was jagged. "It might be important. I better get it."

Jody caught her breath and threw herself back on the bed. "Okay. Hurry!"

Meg dashed into the living room and picked up the phone. "Hello!" Her voice thinly veiled her annoyance at being interrupted.

"Did I catch you at a bad time?" a familiar voice came over the line.

"Well, more like a good time. Never mind! What's up, Marty?"

"I have some bad news, Meg. When the police went to question Patricia today, she was gone, and no one seems to know where she is."

"Oh, hell! What does that mean?"

"Unless they find her, it's going to be much harder trying to prove Jody's innocence, even with the fingerprints. It looks like we're back in the waiting game."

"Oh, shit. Thanks for calling, Marty. Keep us posted." Meg hung up, not wanting to go back to the bedroom. Shoulders slumped, feet dragging, she returned with a heavy tread. Her body relayed the news even before she spoke.

Jody grabbed Meg's hand. "What went wrong?"

"Patricia split, and the police can't find her. If they can't locate her, the trial's still on." Meg sat down on the bed, dejected, defeated.

"Damn, damn, damn, damn! When will it end? When will I get my life back?"

Meg had no answers; all she could do was reach out to Jody. But Jody pushed her away. "Leave me alone, Meg. I just need to be alone." Her heart aching, Meg left Jody and curled up on the couch.

27

A Night on the Town

Somehow, Meg and Jody got through the next couple of weeks. Jody was depleted, withdrawn, sleepwalking, and Meg didn't know how to wake her. They still slept together, drawing comfort from each other's presence, but neither seemed capable of sexual energy.

Every day, Jody was in contact with Marty, asking if there were any leads to Patricia's whereabouts, hoping something would turn up before the trial date, only a month away.

Up early Saturday morning, another bleak day in front of her, Meg sat down with a cup of coffee to read the Portland lesbian-gay paper. On impulse, she turned to the calendar of events, looking for activities for the coming week. "Lesbian Family Workshop." It looked interesting, but it was scheduled for that evening. Meg had often fantasized having her youngest, Stacey, live with her. Her visits home had been all but nonexistent since Jody had come to live with her, and Jody's predicament had precluded any visits from her kids. A workshop like this would be a good opportunity to think through her options and maybe discover Jody's feelings about kids.

Pouring a cup of coffee for Jody, Meg walked up to the bed. Sitting down gingerly, she shook Jody awake. "Time to get up, Jody. We're going into town this afternoon. It's time to get out of here and do something fun for a change."

Jody's voice was muffled by the pillow. "I don't want to go anywhere."

With newly claimed authority, Meg pulled the covers back. "That's too bad, because you're going anyway."

Taking charge, Meg had Jody in the truck within two hours, ignoring her protests. They took their time going to town. Stopping at Lawrence Gallery along the way, they ate at the gourmet restaurant. Meg kept trying to break through the lethargy that had engulfed them for so long. Jody seemed like a sleepwalker, although Meg tried to keep up a constant banter.

They were both hungry again by the time they got to Portland, so Meg drove over to Chin Yen's on East Burnside for a meal of Szechuan chicken and fried eggplant, then on to the meeting at the Unitarian Church. Picketers were out in force, marching militantly back and forth, thrusting their homemade signs in people's faces. "Lesbians can't have children," "Perverts, go home!" and "Save our kids!" predominated.

Jody was in such a fog, she didn't even seem to notice. Meg, more resigned than angry, had to take Jody's arm to lead her through the crowd. "They're everywhere now. I guess we just have to put on our hip boots and wade through their garbage."

As they entered the building, Meg noticed several police cars parked across the street, with a couple of policemen on the edge of the crowd, as if they were anticipating trouble. The trouble for Meg was that she wasn't really sure anymore that she could trust the police to protect her. Their reputation among gays in Portland was laissez-faire at best.

It was almost 7:00 before they found two seats way in the back. The large auditorium was packed. Meg nodded to a couple of acquaintances, but then turned her attention to the program. It was full of good workshops: "Lesbians and the Law," "Co-parenting," "How to Make Your Own Baby," "Homophobia and Your Children," "Adoption: Agencies or Do-It-Yourself?"

As the main speaker began talking, the chants outside grew stronger and shriller. "Dykes, go home!"

"Protect our kids!"

"Damn them!" Meg cursed under her breath. "Who do they think they are? They don't know a thing about me or my family. Who the hell gave them the right to judge me? Jody, I think I want to go to the one on homophobia and kids. What about you?"

"Okay. That sounds fine," Jody answered in a flat voice.

The evening was not going as Meg had hoped, but she was there and planned on learning something. Grabbing Jody's arm, she negotiated their way through the crowd, finding the room down the hall. First, they watched the film

"Sticks and Stones," then broke into small groups to share their experiences with their own kids. Meg found it exciting and challenging, but Jody just sat there looking drugged.

At the break, Meg turned to her. "Come on, we're going outside for a breath of air. You look like you could use some."

Obediently, Jody rose, and they opened the side door, out of sight of the protesters, though their chanting could still be heard. Meg spoke. "Come on, let's walk around the block. It will do us good." The night air was crisp and cool, the sky clear, the moon full. In a few minutes, they rounded the corner. Meg stopped suddenly.

"What's the matter, Meg?"

"I'm not sure, but I think I see someone I know. I'd like to check it out. Walk in front of me and shield me. If I'm right, she might recognize me."

As they drew abreast of the woman, the hood of her coat pulled tight around her face and waving a hauntingly familiar sign, Meg quickly turned to look in her face. "That's her! That's Patricia!" Meg exclaimed, louder than she had intended.

Patricia turned, her expression a mixture of fear and hate, then bolted toward the crowd, trying to push her way into the middle. Meg impulsively reached out to grab her, coming up with a grip on Patricia's lapel.

Patricia swung back toward her, raking Meg's cheek with her fingernails. Startled, Meg let go, instinctively reaching for her stinging face. That was all the time it took for Patricia to flee into the center of the crowd, now aware of Meg and Jody's unwelcome presence.

Within moments, Meg was shoved to her knees. As she looked up, all she could see filling the night sky were placards waving menacingly in her face. She had to get out. Suddenly, someone grabbed her arm. As she turned to face this new peril, Jody hissed in her ear. "It's me, Meg. Let's make tracks." She needed no further encouragement. With Jody's help, she managed to struggle to her feet. Arms linked, they pushed their way to the edge of the crowd and ran across the street.

"Damn! We had her for a minute, Jody. I'm so sorry." Meg faced Jody under a street light, blood trickling unnoticed down her face.

Jody reached out, using the sleeve of her jacket to wipe Meg's face clean. "It's okay, Meg. At least, we know she's still in the area. Let's get you inside and clean you up."

"No! Damn it, Jody. There has to be something we can do. Hey, wait a minute! The last time I saw her at the clinic she was in that weird car whose driver harassed my son. You know, the one covered with bumper stickers I told you about. Maybe she's using it tonight. The police are just on the lookout for her car, not that one. Let's get the truck and cruise around and see what we can find."

"Okay, Meg. It's worth a try. But not for long. Your face needs attention. I wouldn't be surprised if that bitch has rabies."

It took them only a minute to get to the truck, their adrenalin still pumping from the narrow escape from the crowd, whose chanting they could still hear in the background. It felt wonderful to Meg to be in her own truck, the doors locked, the windows only partially down, just in case of another attack.

"Okay, let's think this through, Meg. She probably parked at least three or four blocks away. Let's take the next right, look in both directions every time we pass a street and just start spiraling out as fast as we can. If she's still here, we won't have any trouble spotting her car, even in the dark."

"Sounds good, Jody. You look. I need to concentrate on my driving." With that, Meg accelerated, hoping all the law enforcement officers were still at the demonstration. The darkness pressed in on them; the quiet night was punctuated only by an occasional barking dog.

Meg was just about to make a turn when Jody called out. "Watch out, Meg! To your left!"

As Meg turned, she saw a car without headlights coming at her out of an alley lined with garbage cans. It careened across the street, narrowly missing her bumper, then accelerated down the road.

"That's her! That's the car!" Jody shouted. "Let's go!"

Soon, Meg was almost bumper to bumper with the car. That wasn't so hard. But, now what? She didn't have a car phone. She couldn't very well pull alongside and jump in like a modern-day version of stagecoach melodramas. She didn't have a gun with her and wouldn't be at all surprised if Patricia did. All she could do for now was keep her in sight and hope that something would occur to them when the time came.

In a few minutes, they were in an unfamiliar industrial area. It was getting late. Suddenly, Patricia turned into a large parking lot surrounded by a chainlink fence. Warily, Meg pulled up as close as she dared. The car was scraping the fence as Patricia tried to make a U-turn.

"Hang on, Jody! This is it!" Meg put her foot on the accelerator, closing in. She pushed her fender into the driver's side, taking some satisfaction from Patricia's look of consternation and puzzlement. She kept pushing until the passenger's side was shoved into the fence.

"Good going, pardner." Jody turned to her and smiled. "Looks like she's pinned in. I'll go find a phone and call the police. I can see one on the highway. Stay in the truck. I'll be right back."

Meg and Patricia locked eyes, beyond screaming, beyond talking. The game was up, and Patricia knew it, but the venom still flowed from her body. Meg shivered, refusing nonetheless to turn away, determined to win this final battle of wills.

"Knock! Knock!" Meg jumped, her hands still clutching the steering wheel. "Hey, it's just me, Meg. Let me in." Jody was looking through the window. Meg reached over to unlock the door. "The cops are on their way. They should be here in a couple of minutes."

Just then, Meg spotted the blue and white flashing lights in her rearview mirror. It was the first time in awhile she had been happy to see police.

It wasn't long before Patricia was handcuffed and taken away in a police car, and Meg and Jody were free to go. "Well, we make quite a team," Jody beamed. "Cagney and Lacey, move over! It's time for a celebration, don't you think, pardner?"

Meg couldn't help but laugh. All it took was a car chase in the middle of the night to cheer Jody up. "It's a deal, but first, let's go by a store. I need some antiseptic for my face. It really stings."

"Oh, Meg. I'm sorry. I forgot you had battle scars. Does it hurt a lot? Do you want to go right home?" Jody reached out her hand and gingerly touched Meg's cheek.

"It does sting, but I think a little first aid will fix it up. And no, I don't want to go home yet. I feel like partying. It isn't every day we get a chance to catch a murderer singlehandedly."

They picked up gauze, bandages, iodine and salve at a Safeway, then did a patch-up job in the store's bathroom. Feeling rakish with a gauze patch on her cheek, Meg drove over to Old Wives' Tales. "The sky's the limit! Order anything you want."

The decided to split a couple of orders of chicken and vegetables with peanut sauce and black bean enchiladas with guacamole, with chocolate cake a la mode for dessert. Their energy was high, drawing stares from other customers. Their talk kept spilling over into each other's.

"Did you see her face when she turned on me?"

"I thought the crowd was going to beat us up."

Basking in their newly found freedom from tension, they hardly noticed the waiters cleaning up for the night. They could have sat there, talking and laughing, until the early hours of the morning.

A young waiter with long hair tied neatly at his neck, finally interrupted them. "Excuse me, but we need to mop the floor now. It's past closing. Can I get you your check?"

Meg glanced at the wall clock. Ten thirty-five! They had sat together, oblivious to the other patrons' departures for over a half-hour after closing.

Embarrassed by her lack of awareness and suddenly self-conscious of the dressing on her face, Meg took the check. "Thanks. I guess we better get going."

Leaving a generous five-dollar tip on the table, she and Jody walked out into the nearly deserted parking lot.

As they walked towards the truck, Meg turned to Jody. "Are you ready to go home yet? I'm probably good for another couple of hours."

Jody looked at her, a new hunger in her eyes. "I want to be just with you, Meg. I want to go home and take you in my arms and finish what we began two weeks ago."

Meg stopped in her tracks. She had spent the afternoon as social director and the evening as victorious warrior, both roles she was comfortable with. But that wasn't all she wanted with Jody.

After only a moment's hesitation, she held out her arms, drawing Jody towards her. "Yes, let's go home. It's time."

JUST OUT
P.O. Box 15117
Portland, OR 97215

Attn: Ariel Waterwoman,

Enclosed find a complimentary copy
of my first lesbian detective novel,
A Ship in the Harbor. The setting is
Portland and Lincoln City and Newport,
with much of the action taking place at
Old wives' Tales, Cotton Cloud Futon, and
two downtown women's health clinics.

Mary Heron Dyer
519 NW 11, #5
Corvallis
OR 97330
(503) 752-6857

story, and, lastly, a politically rich detective story that deals directly with the OCA and events such as the Measure 8 campaign a few years ago.

I hope that you enjoy it and see fit to do a book review. I can be reached at the above address and phone number.

Regards and best wishes for the new year.

Mary Heron Dyer

28
A Ship in the Harbor

The ride home was a silent study in mounting desire. Jody's hands slid back and forth along Meg's thigh with a deliberate, slow insistence. From time to time, Meg took her own hand off the wheel to run her finger languidly along Jody's neck.

It was after midnight when they pulled up at the cabin. In a flash, Jody was out of the cab, opening Meg's door, reaching for her, half-helping, half-pulling her into the night, pressing her hard against the cold metal, hungrily finding her lips. Meg's knees almost buckled; she grasped Jody's shoulders, ran her hands down her taut back, as she caressed the tender bare skin where the small of Jody's back disappeared into her tight, low-riding jeans.

Jody threw her head back, drinking in the chill autumn night air in gasps. "Look, Meg." She gestured overhead. Meg laid back against the cab and looked up at the sharp, clear stars. Her mind seemed to stand still at this precious, perfect moment. They held each other gently, breathing together, before stumbling, totally intoxicated, toward the door.

Inside, Meg's shyness, masked as pragmatism, took over. "It's been a long day . . . I wouldn't mind a bath . . . a quick one."

"I'll be here," Jody whispered in her ear.

Fifteen minutes later, in clean jeans and shirt, hair damp, Meg was back.

Candles flickered on the mantel; a newly lit fire flared and crackled. Meg paused in the doorway, amazed at the prowess of an Amazon in heat. Jody stood against the hearth, facing Meg. She held out a wine glass. The top buttons of her shirt were undone, the light blue material framing the pale silken skin between her breasts. Her lips were unsmiling, her eyes intense as a young sea hawk's.

Meg took the glass—deep red, sparkling grape juice. The fire was hot on her cheeks. She lifted the glass, never taking her eyes from Jody's. They drank a silent toast to Eros, bursting free. Slowly, Jody took Meg's glass, put it with hers on the mantel, and led Meg to the couch.

Had Meg ever felt plump? Tonight, she was voluptuous. She sat on the couch, pulling Jody down onto her lap, facing her. Jody's hands ran down the back of Meg's neck, her lips nibbled the hair on the top of Meg's head, her breasts nestled softly against Meg's lips and eyelids. Meg's hands slid up the soft blue material along the outside of those firm, high breasts, her lips planting breathless kisses between them until Jody bent and kissed her, slipping her tongue almost harshly between Meg's lips.

"I want you, Meg." Their bodies exuded a moist heat, damp cheek against damp cheek.

"I've always wanted you, Jody." Meg's voice, trembling, was hardly a whisper.

"I know."

Jody was unbuttoning her own jeans; they rode lower on her hips, blond pubic hair curling out of the open fly.

"What happened to my shy hermit crab?" Meg gasped, her last words as Jody pulled the two of them down onto the long couch.

Jody was busy lifting Meg's sweatshirt, taking a full breast in her hand like a lush tropical fruit, brushing the nipple with her lips.

"Meg," she murmured, "Meg, . . . didn't I tell you? I'm really Jekyll and Hyde. I go crazy in bed . . ." She was on top of Meg now, her leg between Meg's her hips thrusting hard. "Guess I should have told you."

Meg's moans drowned the words. Their breasts touched, melded, pulled away; their nipples were tight, aching, twin points of fire. Their bodies danced in energy rhythms beyond thought, clothes shed like old snake skins, tossed, thrown, dropped around the couch. Flesh found flesh, moist, urgent, hungry. It had been a long wait.

With passionate insistence, lips sought lips, exploring hands found mountains and crevices. Higher and higher, sparse mountain air, distant peaks, gasping for breath. Deeper and deeper, swirling currents, edge of the waterfall, falling, faster, faster, sucked under together, plunging, drowning. Now!

Finally, the release, the exhilaration of conquest and surrender as seeker and quest became one.

The fire had burned down to embers, the candles had guttered. Peace pervaded the room. Crying softly, Meg tried to explain. "It's so hard for me to open myself to someone sexually. I like making love, but to let anyone see me, to trust someone enough to have an orgasm . . . I never even had one with my husband, and we were married for over 15 years."

Jody looked down at her. "Well, then, I'm especially honored. It's all right, you know. You're safe with me."

"I know that. I can feel it." She kissed Jody's neck. They were on the floor, on the rug in front of the fire. Some time, somehow, they had gotten there.

"We have a nice big bed, you know . . ."

In the bed, they curled around each other. "Will you hold me until I fall asleep?" Meg asked, physically sated, emotionally bare, open, newborn.

"Put your head on my breast, and I'll keep my arms around you. How's that?"

Meg nestled against those small, soft pillows, now her own safe haven, and fell asleep.

Meg opened her eyes; dawn's soft light filtered through the window. What had woken her? The phone rang again. As though in a dream, she disengaged herself from Jody and picked up the phone. "Hello?"

The other voice laughed. "Did I interrupt something?"

"Oh, hi, Marty. Yeah, you did interrupt something."

"Good. It's about time. And what I have to tell you is a surprise. Go outside and get your newspaper. Bye."

"Marty, . . ." Too late. She had already hung up.

So Meg, still naked, opened the front door. The paper was under the right front wheel of the truck, a few feet from the door. Glancing around quickly, she made a dash for it. Back in the house, she opened the paper to see the headlines: Pro-Life Activist Confesses to Murder of Lesbian."

"Jody! It's over! She confessed!"

Jody was instantly alert. "Come on in here and read it to me, Woman."

Sitting down on the edge of the bed, Meg began.

"Late last evening, authorities apprehended Patricia Johnston, wanted for questioning in the death of Susan Callahan. After being read her rights and declining the advice of her attorney, Johnston issued the following statement:

"'I went down to the beach to take a day off and relax, and there were queers everywhere. I finally got so upset I had to leave. What's the world coming to when a decent person can't even have a nice day at the beach? They have no right to be in public like that. I didn't go there to be stuck in the middle of a bunch of perverts. When I got so nauseated I had to leave, I could hardly squeeze into my car. They had hemmed me in on both sides. Their cars were disgusting—an old van and an old pickup truck next to it.

"'When I saw the bumper stickers plastered all over the back of those pervert cars, things like "We're everywhere," "Born again pagan," that was when I heard the voice: "Though a thousand fall at your right side, ten thousand at your left, you alone remain unscathed." Then I realized I had been chosen.

"'So I took out the wire cutters I had in my bag for my beadwork. The van was unlocked; it was easy to get inside to the hood release. The other one was locked, but my duty had been set before me, and Satan couldn't stop me. The hood was just held down with wire, and I gave thanks and undid that wire really carefully, so the perverts wouldn't know until it was too late.

"'I cut the brake cables on both those abominable-in-the-sight-of-the-Lord cars. I had a knife in my bag, too. I stabbed one of the tires'"—Meg gasped—"'I would have done the rest too, but somebody came along. So it was in the hands of the Lord. If He had wanted it, nothing would have happened to her. But He chose to kill her. He passed righteous judgment, and He saw that she deserved to die. The Lord used me as His handmaiden. He used me to help rid the earth of the pervert scourge. One is gone, more will follow.'"

As Meg read the last paragraph, tears started down Jody's cheeks. "Meg, how could anyone wish anyone else a death like Susan's?"

Meg reached out to put a hand on Jody's leg. "Do you want me to stop reading?"

"No. I want to hear all of it."

"Okay. There isn't much left.

"When asked for a comment on the unexpected confession, the District Attorney stated, 'In light of this statement, we will request a full psychiatric examination. Until then, we will not be filing charges, but if the facts corroborate Johnston's story, the charges against Jody Miller will be dropped by the end of the week.'

"When a reporter from a gay newspaper asked Johnston why she hated homosexuals so much, she refused to answer. He pressed further. 'Isn't it true that you have a gay son from whom you are estranged?'

"She replied, 'That's a vicious lie! He'll come around if you just leave him alone! I didn't raise my son to be a pervert. I raised him in a good, Christian, God-fearing home.'

"Refusing to answer any more questions, Johnston was escorted back to jail. A bail hearing is set for the morning."

"Well, Meg, the waiting's over." Jody wiped her eyes and ran her hands through her hair, now sticking up in blond spikes. "I guess it's time to pick up the pieces of my life."

Meg's stomach contracted into a tight ball. "You know, you're welcome to stay here for as long as you like, Jody."

"I know that, Meg." She ran her hand slowly up and down Meg's arm. "You've been wonderful. Goddess, how wonderful!" She kissed Meg softly on the cheek. "But I need some time to myself. I still feel so confused . . . I've been so busy trying to convince everyone I didn't kill Susan I haven't had time to mourn for her. Or for myself." Her voice was soft. "I did love her once, you know . . . and in the deepest ways, I never stopped loving her. I have to find a way to say goodbye, to set her free. To set myself free." She took a deep breath. "I think I love you, but I don't think either of us knows if we were just thrown together by fate, or if we're really meant to be together."

Meg sighed, her heart breaking. All her self-doubt flooded back. But Jody was right, as hard as it was to hear it. "Jody, it's been wonderful having you here. There's a part of me that wants you to just keep living here, everything just the same. But I probably need some time, too." Meg paused, then drew back, unconsciously putting distance between them. "Do you feel ready to go home now? Would you like a cup of coffee before you go?"

Jody leaned over, drawing Meg to her. "It's going to be all right, Meg. I just need some time to sort things out. I'll call you tomorrow. I do love you, you know."

Meg tried to smile. "Yeah . . . well." Resolutely, she pushed herself up. "Why don't I make some more coffee while you get your things together?"

On the way to the kitchen, Meg checked on yesterday's mail, mostly just to get out of the cabin a moment, to pull herself together. Back inside, she tossed the mail onto the kitchen counter and busied herself making a fresh pot of coffee, not trusting herself to watch Jody erase the endearing clutter she'd scattered through the cabin.

It wasn't long before Jody stuck her head through the kitchen door. "I'll pass on the coffee. I love you, Meg. I'll call you tomorrow."

Moments later, Meg heard the front door close softly. "I love you, too, Jody," she murmured.

Meg sat there, hunched over her coffee, lacking the energy to do anything, even get breakfast. Was it all a dream? Was she just a handy port in Jody's storm? Was she all alone again? What was she going to do with her life without wrapping her dreams up in Jody? Meg wasn't even sure if Mrs. Green could keep her through the winter, with the summer trade gone.

It was late morning before she was able to rouse herself, her coffee grown cold. She began idly leafing through the mail—just some circulars and a note from Lloyd, probably asking her to do some job around the cabins. "Meg, sorry for such short notice, but my father just died, and I had to fly back east. I've inherited his business and will probably have to relocate."

Meg drew in her breath. "Oh, no," she moaned out loud. "Where will I move to that I can afford?"

The note continued. "If I do move, I don't want to sell the cabins. I was hoping you'd consider managing them. I could pay you 15-20% of the rent you could bring in. Think it over. I'll be back next week. We can talk then. Lloyd."

Meg poured herself another cup of coffee, taking it out to her thinking place on the back steps. What would it be like to be the manager, instead of the caretaker? She had honed her skills enough in the last few months to feel confident to do most of the repairs on her own. That wouldn't be the problem.

It would be dealing with all kinds of people, some of them arrogant male jerks. She wasn't sure she was up to that.

But what if she just advertised in the gay paper? Something like: "Weekend and vacation rentals for women. Ocean view. Group rates available." Now that was an idea! Lloyd wouldn't care. Actually, Lloyd wouldn't have to know, as long as she kept them rented.

The Lavender Harbor . . . that's what she would call it. She could see it now, a place to come to be protected and sheltered and loved—a real place, not just a place in a child's lullaby. Come to think of it, there was an old piece of marine plywood out back just the right size for a sign, and there was plenty of paint around. She got up suddenly, knocking over her coffee.

The afternoon passed quickly, Meg humming Cris Williamson's lullaby over and over again as the sign took shape between her paint-covered hands. Finally, stepping back to admire her handiwork, Meg remembered the Quaker saying, "Way will open." When some doors closed, others opened—sometimes, even when one's faith had been misplaced or lost.

The late afternoon shade was overtaking her work area. As Meg picked up the sign and took it around to the southwestern side of the cabin, she noticed the mailbox was partially open. After she had put down the sign, she checked the mail. Normally, she was cued in to the arrival of the mailtruck, but she had been so busy with her new project she must not have heard it.

Putting her hand in the box, she pulled out some circulars, then felt something on the bottom, a wadded up piece of paper with something inside. Puzzled, she pulled it out. There lay a cowrie shell, burnished chestnut oval top, rich cream edges. She remembered it well; it had been Jody's special find that day they had first met and walked on the beach. "This always reminded me of you, Meg," the note said. "Now let it keep me in your heart."

It just fit in the palm of Meg's hand. She went back inside the cabin, holding it tight. Inside, she placed the shell carefully, reverently, on the mantel next to the two wine glasses from the previous night. Then she took the wine glasses to the kitchen, suddenly whistling, aware of a ravenous appetite. She built herself a sandwich of everything she could find, poured herself the remains of the sparkling grape juice, and went back outside for one last look at the sign. The sun was setting, the orange sky showing just a hint of lavender, glinting off the still wet paint.

Acknowledging the sun as it dipped into the ocean, Meg raised her glass. "I claim this place for myself, for those I love, and for women who need a refuge in the storm. And for Jody, my love, . . . may your complete you journey safely and soon."

Softly at first, then with growing strength, Meg started singing, waves lapping at her feet in accompaniment.

> "Like a ship in the harbor,
> Like a mother and child,
> Like a light in the darkness,
> I'll hold you awhile.

> "We'll rock on the water,
> I'll cradle you deep,
> And hold you while angels
> Sing you to sleep."

About the Author

Mary Heron Dyer, who makes her home in Western Oregon, is a political activist and therapist who works with women and children who are survivors of domestic and sexual violence. She dreams about and works toward the day when the violence will be over and she will have more time for her lover, her family and friends, her garden, and her writing.